BREAKAWAY

W.C. Mack

Cover by
Paul Perreault

Scholastic Canada Ltd.
Toronto New York London Auckland Sydney
Mexico City New Delhi Hong Kong Buenos Aires

Scholastic Canada Ltd.
604 King Street West, Toronto, Ontario M5V 1E1, Canada

Scholastic Inc.
557 Broadway, New York, NY 10012, USA

Scholastic Australia Pty Limited
PO Box 579, Gosford, NSW 2250, Australia

Scholastic New Zealand Limited
Private Bag 94407, Botany, Manukau 2163, New Zealand

Scholastic Children's Books
Euston House, 24 Eversholt Street, London NW1 1DB, UK

www.scholastic.ca

Library and Archives Canada Cataloguing in Publication
Mack, Winnie, 1972-
Breakaway / W.C. Mack.
ISBN 978-1-4431-1942-9
I. Title.
PS8625.A24B74 2012   jC813'.6   C2012-904927-1

6 5 4 3 2 1   Printed in Canada 121   12 13 14 15 16

For my nephew, the mighty Max,
and his Uncle Mike.
— W.C.M

Chapter One

Everything was going my way as I headed for the goal, as if I was daydreaming instead of right there, in person.

I deked out Colin Bechter, then Patrick Chen, in like, two seconds flat. No problem at all.

When I got within shooting distance I couldn't help smiling when I saw David "Bedhead" McCafferty bouncing from one foot to the other, trying to look ready.

But trying to look ready and actually being ready are two totally different things.

And Bedhead wasn't ready for me.

At that moment, Roberto Luongo wouldn't have been ready for me.

I hummed to myself as I lined up the shot. All Bedhead would see was a blur of orange when the ball flew past him and into the net. (Hopefully, it wouldn't go too far, though. We were on the last ball of the six-pack from my garage.)

I pulled my stick back, remembering the roar of the loudest Cougar fans at the last game before the holidays.

I wished we were playing at the Rogers Centre.

I wished my hoodie was a Canucks jersey.

I wished it was a real game.

"Car!" Kenny Cavanaugh shouted.

But most of all, I wished we weren't playing on Daffodil Drive.

I groaned as Colin and Bedhead lifted Kenny's junker net off the road so a Honda could squeeze by us.

The lady who was driving waved and honked her horn a couple of times to say thank you.

"No problem," I sighed, waving back.

But it *was* a problem. A million-in-one shot like that wasn't going to happen again any time soon. My huge (well, big, anyway) moment was gone.

"Why don't we move to Primrose?" Patrick suggested. "Less traffic."

"Less flat," Colin reminded him. "We'll spend the whole game digging the ball out of the ditch."

"What about Bluebell?" Kenny asked.

"What about a thousand potholes?" Colin answered.

It was more like four or five, but I knew what he meant. Bluebell Lane was a mess.

Jeff McDaniel rested his chin on the handle of his stick. "We should play in the mall parking lot."

"Seriously?" I stared at him. "On Christmas Eve?"

He groaned. "Oh, yeah. I forgot."

Who could forget about Christmas, for crying out loud?

"Can you imagine how many people are down there right now?" Patrick asked. "I bet that place is packed."

I shook my head, hoping that at least one of the last-minute shoppers was my sister Wendy, buying me the Canucks history book I'd put at the top of my wish list.

Unlike Jeff, *I* hadn't forgotten about Christmas, but I

wasn't nearly as excited as I usually was. Any other year, I would have wanted Christmas Day to last a whole week, but winter hockey camp was starting on Boxing Day and I was counting the minutes.

And sometimes the seconds.

I'd been looking forward to camp since October, when I'd spotted a sign on the bulletin board down at the rink. As I read the big blue letters and my mouth dropped open with shock (and possibly a drip or two of drool), I was glad Eddie Bosko hadn't been around to call me a flounder.

And the more I read, the lower my jaw dropped, because this wasn't any old hockey camp.

The coach was Danny Holbrook, a retired Vancouver Canuck.

He'd played before I was born, back in the nineties, and I didn't know as much about him as I did about the stars like Pavel Bure and Russ Courtnall. But I didn't care (too much, anyway) because whether he was a star or not, he'd been a pro, from my favourite team!

If my parents would send me, I, Nugget McDonald, would have the chance to learn some new moves from an NHL pro.

And how awesome was that? (That is what my English teacher calls a rhetorical question. It doesn't need an answer because everyone knows it's, like, the most awesome thing ever.)

When I told Mum and Dad about the camp that afternoon, they thought about it for longer than they needed to (like, five whole minutes!) and finally, when I didn't think I could take the waiting anymore, they told me I could go. From that moment on, I'd been marking a big red X on my calendar every night before I went to bed.

And there was only one more X to go.

I watched the guys move the net back into place and as soon as Bedhead nodded I dropped the ball, ready to rock Daffodil Drive.

I moved the ball down the asphalt as fast as I could, knowing Kenny was right on my tail. Colin came at me from the left and tried to check me, but he didn't stand a chance. With some fancy footwork and a solid shoulder, I left him with a view of my back.

Bedhead looked even more nervous than last time and I couldn't wait to fire the ball right past him.

"It came!" someone shouted from behind me.

I spun around and saw one of the Watson triplets running toward us. He was wearing one of the biggest smiles I'd ever seen and waving something in the air.

My moment wasn't going to be ruined again. I turned back to the ball.

"What came?" Bedhead asked, stepping away from the net.

"Nothing as important as what I'm sending you right now," I told him.

"My Holbrook jersey!" the triplet shouted.

What?

That stopped me. In fact, I tripped over my own feet trying to turn around.

We all checked out the jersey he was holding up to his chest. The logo on the front was a pair of white hockey sticks, crossed, with a green box around them and the name "Holbrook's Heroes" above it.

The colours were pure Canuck.

Before I could ask where he got it, he turned around and showed us the back, which had "Holbrook" across the top.

"Shouldn't it say Watson on the back?" Patrick asked me.

"I think it's awesome," I whispered back.

A personalized jersey from Danny Holbrook.

I couldn't believe it.

"I got mine yesterday," Kenny said.

What?

"No way! Where did you get it?" I asked, already dying to have one of my own.

"In the mail." Kenny paused for a second, looking confused. "You didn't get one?"

"No," I told him, shaking my head slowly. "Was I supposed to?"

"Yeah," Bedhead said. "Mine got here on Thursday."

"Mine, too," Colin said.

"I didn't get one." My hands were starting to sweat. "Yet."

"Your mum signed you up for camp, didn't she?" Kenny asked, looking worried.

"Duh," I said, rolling my eyes. "We've only been talking about it for two months."

"Well, you should have gotten a jersey, then."

"So where is it?"

Kenny shrugged. "Maybe it'll come tomorrow."

I shook my head. "No mail on Christmas."

Nuts! I wanted to wear my jersey on the first day of camp, just like everyone else.

Why hadn't it shown up earlier in the week? Was it lost in the mail? Did someone steal it from our doorstep?

I had to find the answer.

I had to find that jersey.

Right away.

"I gotta go," I told Kenny, turning back toward my house.

"Where are you going?"

I didn't bother answering, even when I heard the rest of the Cutter Bay Cougars shouting after me to come back and play.

When I opened the kitchen door, Mum was sitting at the table, wearing the purple sweater Wendy and I went in together on for her birthday. I was glad to see she was using it, but I had way more important things on my mind.

"I'm surprised to see you already," she said with a laugh. "Did you forget your puck?"

"We use a ball for street hockey," I reminded her. "And no." As if that would ever happen. "Hey, did something come in the mail for me?" I asked.

She smiled. "A couple of packages did, but I've hidden them away for tomorrow."

"But I need to see —"

Mum shook her head. "Nope. You know, you've always been the worst for trying to sneak a peek at Christmas presents, Nugget."

"This isn't about Christmas," I said, sounding a bit ruder than I meant to. But I couldn't help it! This was an emergency! "Can I just see the packages?"

She frowned at me. "What's going on?"

I pictured the Holbrook jersey in my head.

Man, I wanted one. Like, last Tuesday.

"The guys all got jerseys in the mail. For hockey camp," I told her. "Did I get one?"

Mum frowned. "No, you have a package from Grandpa Charlie and another from Auntie Carol and Uncle Mike."

"Nothing else?" I asked.

"No," she said. "But I paid the registration fee when I signed you up, so I'm sure yours is coming."

I nodded and tried to breathe normally. "Yeah, because that was way back in October." Plenty of time.

"Actually, I think it was closer to the end of November." What?

"November?" I'd told her about the camp the same day I saw the sign, and that was *definitely* the beginning of October.

My heart started pounding like I'd been skating lines for twenty minutes.

Something had gone wrong. I just knew it.

"Look, it's not going to matter whether I registered you in October or November, honey. If the camp comes with a jersey, you'll get one."

I wanted to believe her, but I had a gut feeling that it wasn't going to be that simple.

"Are you sure you waited that long?" I asked, wondering what the heck she'd been waiting *for*.

"Let me grab my chequebook," Mum said, leaving the kitchen.

I thought about my calendar, covered with X's, and all the time I'd spent imagining ways to impress Danny Holbrook. What if Mum had made a mistake and I wasn't even registered? I couldn't spend the whole Christmas break taking shots against the garage by myself.

Maybe I could head down to the rink in the morning and talk my way in? Or was it too late? Was I going to miss out on the coolest camp Cutter Bay had ever seen?

Mum was back in a couple of minutes, waving her chequebook. "Here we go. November nineteenth. Made out to the Holiday Hockey Challenge."

I let out a sigh of relief. "Whew!"

Everything was going to be okay.

At least I *thought* it was.

*   *   *

Christmas morning was pretty awesome. My sister and I didn't wake up at six o'clock the way we used to when we were little, but we were ready for action by eight.

As usual, it was almost impossible to sit through a French toast breakfast, watching Mum and Dad sip coffee as slowly as they could, before we hit the living room to open presents.

But it was worth the wait, because I got practically everything on my list. Wendy gave me the book I'd been dying to add to my hockey library, and my new gear bag (with the old-school Canucks logo on it) was the coolest one I'd ever seen. And the framed Jean Ducette rookie card from Grandpa Charlie? Seriously awesome.

My family seemed pretty happy with the presents I got for them, too. Mum and Dad both started using their new coffee mugs practically as soon as they opened them and Wendy actually hugged me when she saw the iTunes card I'd given her.

Not that I liked it or anything, but it was better than the noogie or eye roll she gave me every other day of the year.

Once we were finished opening presents and folding wrapping paper so Mum could use it again next year, the rain started. Of course, I wouldn't have been allowed to play hockey with the guys on Christmas Day anyway, but it would have been nice to try out the new stick from Mum and Dad in the driveway or something. But it seriously poured for hours, so the McDonald family read, watched a movie on TV and ate a gravy-drenched turkey dinner. Then it was time for board games.

I checked my watch and saw that it was seven o'clock. Just a few more hours until hockey camp.

"Just one more night," I whispered.

"Until you roll the stupid dice?" Wendy snapped.

Huh?

"Jonathan?" Mum said. "Are you still with us?"

I shook myself out of my daydream and realized it was my turn in our annual Christmas Monopoly marathon.

"He's on another planet," Wendy said, rolling her eyes. "Planet of the geeks."

I guess she'd already forgotten about that iTunes card. "Better than planet of the freaks," I told her, reaching for the dice.

"It's Christmas," Mum reminded us with a sigh. "Can we please take a little holiday from bickering?"

I rolled a seven and landed on Park Place.

Great.

"Ha!" Wendy shrieked. "You owe me . . . " she checked the card and counted the buildings on her property. She'd maxed it out with a hotel. "Fifteen hundred dollars." She smirked. "Pay up."

I glanced at my bank, which had way more ten and one dollar bills than anything else.

"Uh . . . can I owe you?"

She shook her head. "You already owe me two hundred dollars."

"But —"

"You're going to have to go bankrupt, Nugget." She snickered. "It's game over for you."

"It's Christmas," I reminded her.

"So?"

"So, why are you being such a creep?"

"Excuse me?"

"Okay," Dad said. "Let's try to end the day on a high note."

"Yes, this has been a lovely Christmas," Mum said, looking from me to my sister. "Thanks, you two."

I didn't think I could go after Wendy while Mum had happy tears in her eyes. I also didn't have a chance to find out, because the doorbell rang.

"Who on earth could that be?" Mum asked, looking annoyed.

I had a pretty good idea who it was, and I turned out to be right. When I opened the front door, Kenny Cavanaugh was standing there, his usual Red Wings tuque on his head.

"How's it going?" he asked.

I knew how Mum felt about Christmas being family time, so I tried to make the visit quick. I told him about all the cool presents I got and promised to show him the Ducette card later.

"A rookie card?" he said. "That has to be the coolest thing in your collection."

I stared at him. "Sure, Kenny. Except for the signed Ducette jersey on my wall. You know, the one he signed *while I was wearing it*."

It was only the greatest moment of my life.

"Oh yeah," he said. "I always forget about that."

I never did. Meeting my favourite Canuck was the most awesome thing that had ever happened to me. And I was going to meet another one the very next day!

Danny Holbrook, here I come!

"Hey, what about you?" I asked.

"What about me?"

"Christmas, Kenny. What did you get?"

He frowned, like he was thinking really hard. "A couple of sweaters, a fish puzzle with like two thousand pieces that looks impossible, a new coat and some socks and underwear."

Ugh.

"Socks and underwear?" I asked. That was the Christmas kiss of death. Worse than school supplies, even.

He shrugged. "I needed some, I guess. My grandma knit the socks."

He pulled up the cuffs of his jeans so I could see the brown wool. "They look . . . warm," I said. And lumpy. And itchy.

"Yeah, my feet are already sweating."

I could imagine, and I didn't want to. "Did you get any *fun* stuff?" I asked.

He nodded. "Some video games. And my uncle from Toronto gave me a toboggan."

We both looked down at the wet pavement, then up at the drizzling sky. As usual, snow seemed like a long shot.

"Cool," I told him.

"Nugget," Dad called from the dining room, "Scrabble starts in two minutes." He paused for a second. "Merry Christmas, Kenny."

"Merry Christmas, Mr. McDonald," Kenny called back, then spoke more quietly. "Okay, I found out why you didn't get a Holbrook jersey."

"Why not?" I asked.

"You guys are on a different team."

"What do you mean, *you guys*?" I asked, then realized there was a more important question. "Wait a second. What other team?"

He shrugged. "They had a lot of kids sign up for hockey camp. Like, kids from Port Alberni *and* here."

"So?" I asked, not sure what that had to do with me.

"So, they brought in another coach."

"Another Canuck?" I asked. What if it was someone more famous than Holbrook, like Stan Smyl or Courtnall? I'd have a heart attack, for sure.

Kenny shook his head. "I've never heard of the guy. It's Gunnar."

"Gunnar?" I repeated, totally confused.

"K. Gunnar," he said.

"Who the heck is K. Gunnar?" I asked.

"Didn't I just say I'd never heard of the guy?" Kenny asked.

I pulled him into the house and shut the door behind him.

"Follow me," I said, heading for the den.

"Whoa," Mum said from the doorway. "Where's the fire?"

I told her about Gunnar, the total unknown.

She shrugged, then patted my shoulder. "Nugget, it's the same rink and the same camp. The only thing that's different is the coach."

"But that's the most important part of it!" I practically choked. "Danny Holbrook was a *Canuck*, for crying out loud. I've never even heard of K. Gunnar."

Who was K. Gunnar?

"Relax," she said, giving the shoulder a squeeze that was supposed to make me feel better. "You're getting too wound up about this. It's going to be fine."

"Maybe it's Gunnar Grimmel," Kenny said, hopefully. "From the Blackhawks."

Not what I wanted to hear. At all.

"I hate the Blackhawks," I groaned. "And Gunnar is the last name, not the first. We've got to check online."

I logged on, typed the name and the words "hockey player," then leaned back in Dad's chair to wait.

It didn't take long for an answer, and when it popped up, I couldn't believe what I read.

Judging by the gasp from Kenny, he was as shocked as I was.

My hockey camp coach wasn't an NHL player.

She was a girl.

Chapter Two

"Katie Gunnar?" I asked Mum as she started the dishwasher. "I can't believe you signed me up for a hockey camp with *Katie Gunnar*!"

"I can't, either, Jonathan," Mum sighed, obviously tired of the conversation that had been going around in circles for about ten minutes.

Kenny had given up after five. Instead of backing me up, he left to have hot chocolate and sing Christmas carols at his place.

I had nothing to sing about. The rest of my teammates were about to start their dream camp while I was headed straight into a nightmare. The whole point of camp was to hang out with a pro!

"Honey," Mum said. "As I've mentioned four or five times now, I am very, very sorry about this. You know that it was a mistake and I wish it hadn't happened." She found room for the milk in our packed fridge.

"I know," I sighed. "It's just —"

"You had your heart set on playing with a Canuck.

Believe me, I understand how disappointed and upset you are."

I could tell she meant what she was saying, and I knew she felt bad. But Mum feeling bad wasn't going to fix the problem.

"Katie Gunnar," I moaned again.

"I don't know what you want me to say, honey. We could cancel, but I'm sure it's too late for a refund. And this camp wasn't cheap."

"I don't want to *cancel*," I groaned. "I just want to play with Danny Holbrook."

"So I hear," Mum said, reaching for a cloth to wipe the counter. "Over and over again."

"What's going on?" Dad asked.

I explained the situation and waited for him to come up with the ultimate solution.

But that didn't happen.

"That's a tough break, Nugget," he said, patting me on the back and giving me a sympathetic smile. "I know how excited you were about camp."

"Not just camp, Dad. Danny Holbrook! He was a —"

"Canuck," he finished for me. "Your number one team. But I'm sure this Katie Gunnar is qualified," he added.

"Qualified?" I choked. "Is she an NHL superstar, Dad?"

"Was Holbrook?" he asked, doubtfully.

He had me there. "Not a superstar, but at least he was a player."

"Katie Gunnar must be a player too," he said.

"Well, considering there are no girls in the NHL, I'm pretty sure she isn't," I told him.

"Good grief," Mum said. "There's more to hockey than the NHL."

"True," Dad said.

"What?" I choked. There was no way on earth he actually agreed with that.

"What do you know about her?" Dad asked.

"That she's a girl who plays hockey." And ruins the lives of eleven-year-old boys who were counting the seconds until hockey camp.

"That's all you and Kenny found online?" Mum asked.

"As soon as I saw what the K stood for, I stopped reading," I explained.

"Very impressive," Mum said. I could tell she was being sarcastic. Years of living with my sister had made me an expert.

"Well," Dad said, "She wouldn't be running a camp if she didn't know what she was doing."

"Exactly," Mum said, like that solved everything.

"This is totally nuts," I sighed. "I can't even believe it's happening."

"What?" Wendy asked, from the doorway. "I thought we were playing Scrabble."

"Mum signed me up for hockey camp with a girl coach instead of Danny Holbrook."

"Who's Danny Holbrook?"

"A former Canuck."

"And?" she asked, checking for chips in her green nail polish.

"He was supposed to be my coach," I told her, crossing my arms. "And now I have a girl coach instead."

My sister snorted and stared at me. "And we're supposed to feel sorry for you?"

I nodded.

"At least you get to go to a hockey camp, Nugget. Think

of all the kids who don't have the chance to do something like that."

"Good point, honey," Mum said, smiling.

Ever since Wendy's volleyball team served an early Christmas meal at a homeless shelter in Victoria, she'd been acting like she was the most charitable person on the planet. And I knew for a fact that she wasn't. I'd played Monopoly with her.

She looked down her nose at me and said, "You don't know how good you have it. That camp is a total luxury. I mean, do you understand that there are starving kids all over the world?"

Why was she trying to make *me* feel bad?

"Yeah, I do. And I doubt starving kids care about going to hockey camp," I reasoned.

As soon as the words were out of my mouth, I wanted to take them back.

"Jonathan," Mum gasped.

"What did you just say?" Dad asked, frowning.

"You know, sometimes I can't even believe I'm related to you," Wendy sneered as she walked out of the room.

"I'm sorry," I told my parents. And I was. I cared about starving people. A lot. But the truth was, I also cared about hockey. "I'm just upset about camp." My Christmas vacation had been totally destroyed. Couldn't they understand that?

"Look, Nugget," Dad said. "You can do one of two things. You can show up for camp tomorrow, ready to learn, or you can sit at home for the rest of your vacation while everyone else is out having fun on the ice."

"With Danny Holbrook," I sighed.

"That's enough," Dad said, his tone letting me know that the conversation was over.

So was game night, it turned out. I'd ruined the mood. On Christmas. We stayed up for a couple more hours, reading and watching TV, but it wasn't the same.

When I got to the point when I couldn't stop yawning, I said goodnight to everyone and left the room. On the way upstairs, I heard Mum say something about selfish children.

Great.

The thing is, I wasn't *trying* to be selfish. I knew that other kids had way bigger problems than me. I knew I was lucky to have parents who took good care of me and were willing to pay for hockey camp.

I just wished they'd paid for the right one.

I flopped on my bed and stared at my Ducette jersey, wishing everything had worked out the way it was supposed to.

Danny Holbrook might not have been the most awesome player in history but he'd made it all the way to the NHL. He'd lived my dream, and I wanted to know what it felt like.

But instead? I had Katie Gunnar.

Of course, I knew that girls could play sports. I mean, my sister was the star of her high school volleyball team. A bunch of the girls in my grade played soccer, too, and I saw how good they were during gym class. And one of the girls who graduated from Cutter Bay High School last year won a big basketball scholarship for some university in the States.

But hockey was something totally different.

Hockey was the game that *guys* loved the most. Me and my dad both played, but Mum and Wendy never did. Hockey was fast, exciting, and sometimes it got a little rough.

How was a girl supposed to teach me how to play against guys?

And what could I possibly learn from Katie Gunnar that I didn't already know?

* * *

The sound of my blaring alarm clock yanked me out of an awesome Stanley Cup dream at six the next morning. I hit the "off" button and closed my eyes, trying to finish the dream with a game-winning goal, but the details had already faded away.

I groaned and rolled out of bed. For a split second, I thought it was a school day. Then I started to smile when I realized it was the first day of hockey camp.

But the smile didn't make it all the way onto my face before I remembered that camp was ruined.

In the shower, the only shampoo we had left was the special strawberry stuff Wendy used. I knew I wasn't supposed to touch it, but I had no choice. As I washed the bubbles out of my hair, I realized that I wasn't only going to be coached by a girl, I was going to smell like one.

Great.

When I'd dried off, I put on my sweatpants and my Canucks hoodie. I'd packed my usual practice jersey in my bag the night before, figuring if there was a Gunnar jersey waiting for me at the rink, I might not want to wear it.

After all, it would probably be pink.

The truth was, I wasn't only disappointed because my coach was a girl instead of a Canuck. It also stunk that while the Cougars played together, I was going to be stuck with a bunch of guys from Port Alberni. Guys we'd played against forever.

The enemy.

I shook my head, wondering how everything had gotten so messed up.

When I made it to the kitchen, Mum handed me a plate of blueberry waffles and told me to go light on the syrup.

As if I could.

"Have we made an attitude adjustment since yesterday?" she asked, slicing chunks of banana onto her cereal.

"Mmmhmm," I lied, through a mouthful of deliciousness.

"I'm glad to hear it. I bet you'll be surprised at how much you enjoy camp."

I nodded. She was right. If I enjoyed it, I would definitely be surprised.

"I think you need to get over this anti-girl nonsense," she said. "In case you've forgotten, I used to be a girl."

"I know," I said, reaching for more syrup.

Mum grabbed the bottle before I could. "And you probably don't believe it, but in a couple of years you'll be looking at girls in a totally new way."

"You're right," I said, then waited until she smiled before I added, "I don't believe it."

Her smile turned into the one she always flashed at me when she thought she knew something that I didn't. "We'll see about that."

We finished our breakfast and I loaded my gear into the van. Mum had made me a "to-go" cup of hot chocolate for the drive to the rink, complete with five tiny melting marshmallows, which made me feel a little better.

Just a little, though.

I sipped while we listened to CBC news, which Mum always liked in the morning. I wouldn't have minded some music to help get me pumped up, but it was driver's choice.

When we got to the rink, I swung my bag onto my back, almost knocking the wind out of myself, and gave Mum a wave goodbye.

"I'll see you later," she said, then called after me, "Have *fun!*"

I walked across the rink's parking lot, almost crushed by the weight of my bag. When I pulled open the front door I took a big sniff. That place smelled more like home to me than my own bedroom.

I thought about all the practice hours I'd spent on the ice and all of the games the Cougars had won and lost under that roof. I remembered how divided the team had been when my dad filled in for Coach O'Neal when he had surgery.

A lot of stuff had happened in that building, good and bad, but the Cougars had made it through together. We were a solid team, for sure.

It was going to feel pretty weird to be on a different team for the next week.

And even more weird to be surrounded by guys from Port Alberni on my own home turf.

I looked around the snack bar, then walked over to the rink, but didn't see any guys I didn't recognize. I figured they were probably all in the Visitors locker room or something. I sure didn't want them in ours.

I turned the corner and saw Patrick Chen down the hall. His bag looked even heavier than mine, but he was way taller than me (just like everybody else) and outweighed me by at least twenty pounds.

"Hey Nugget," he said, when he heard me behind him and turned.

"Hey," I grunted, counting the steps until I could put the bag down.

"Are you pretty excited?" he asked, slowing down so I could catch up.

I laughed and shook my head. "I'm not sure excited is the word."

He squinted at me, like he was confused. "It's hockey camp."

"I know," I said.

"So why aren't you —"

"I'm on Gunnar's team."

I waited for him to either laugh or look sorry for me, but he grinned instead. "Me too."

"You are?" I asked, surprised.

"Yeah. We're teammates, Nugget."

I couldn't help smiling, just a little. I wouldn't be the only Cougar on Gunnar's team, after all. For the first time since I'd found out she was my coach, I started to relax.

"Cool," I told him. "Your mum signed you up late too, eh?"

Patrick's confused look was back. "Late? No, I was registered before they even advertised it."

It was my turn to be confused. "But you're on Gunnar's team?"

He nodded. "Yeah."

"But I thought they only put a second team together when Holbrook's got filled up."

"They did," he said. "And when I heard about it, my mum called them and they let me switch."

What?

"You switched to the *girl*?" I asked, stunned.

He laughed. "I switched to the *gold medalist*."

"What?"

"Katie Gunnar," he said. "Two-time gold medalist for women's hockey."

"But —"

I must have looked as confused as I felt, because he added, "The *Olympics*, Nugget."

"Gold medals?" I frowned. Olympics? Maybe I should have kept reading about Gunnar online.

"Yeah, and you know, Danny Holbrook may have been an NHL player, but he was never MVP."

"MVP?"

"Yup," he said, as we entered the locker room. "Katie Gunnar was MVP."

I barely had a chance for the words to sink in before all of the noise and action in the locker room took over my brain.

Most of the Cougars were already there, half-dressed in their gear and joking around. Almost everybody was wearing a Holbrook's Heroes jersey, which didn't feel quite as bad as it could have, now that I knew Patrick was on my team.

I could smell Jeff's beef jerky breakfast before I even saw it hanging out of his mouth. Bedhead was living up to his nickname, with hair sticking up in every possible direction. When we nodded at each other, it looked like exploding fireworks.

Tim was standing in front of the bench, bouncing a tennis ball on his stick. It was kind of like something I'd seen my grandpa Charlie do with a golf club and ball, but way, way easier.

I high-fived Kenny, Chris Fullerton, Colin and one of the Watson triplets (I'm not sure which one), then spotted Bosko in the corner. He was silent, concentrating on lacing his skates. Most of the guys were still scared of him, but I wasn't (most of the time, anyway), so I dropped my gear on the floor with a thud and sat down next to him.

"Nugget," he said, in a voice that sounded older than my dad.

"How's it going, Bosko?"

"Good," he said, finishing with his laces and pulling his Holbrook jersey out of his bag. He glanced at me. "Have you done your Math homework yet?"

The only things my tutor and I had in common were hockey and Math, and I would have rather stuck to hockey right then. I mean, who really wants to talk about Math homework?

"It's Christmas break," I reminded him, unzipping my bag.

"I know," he grunted. "It was a Christmas break assignment."

"I still have a whole week left," I said, pulling on my shoulder pads.

He raised one eyebrow at me. "And you're going to wait until the end?"

"Well . . . yeah." I adjusted the pads so they fit right.

He shook his head. "I'm not going to be able to help you the night before school starts, Nugget."

"I didn't ask you to."

"Yet," he said, with a smirk.

He strapped on his helmet and told me he'd see me on the ice.

"From a distance, anyway," I muttered.

As I bent over to pull on my skates and tie the laces, I watched all of my buddies laughing and goofing off in their matching jerseys. They were way more excited about camp than I was.

No matter what Patrick said, I couldn't help feeling that MVP of a women's tournament wasn't as cool as MVP of the NHL.

And a couple of gold medals didn't change the fact that Katie Gunnar was a girl.

Chapter Three

When I'd finished getting ready, I headed for the rink with the rest of the guys. They were loud and rowdy, ready for the best week of their lives.

I tried not to be jealous, but it was impossible.

"This is going to be awesome," Chris Fullerton said. "I can't wait to show Holbrook my moves."

"Forget it," Kenny said, laughing. "He's gonna be too busy checking out mine."

"We'll see," Chris laughed, giving him a punch on the shoulder.

Normally, I would have been right in there, telling Kenny he was going to be blinded by my brilliance on the ice or something like that. I would have been elbowing Chris and shoulder-checking Colin as we turned the corner to the rink.

But this wasn't normal. It felt weird, not being part of the excitement, not saying anything.

When we turned the corner, I saw Jeremy Simpson and Curtis Blank, who were both Cougars benchwarmers, walking in front of me. Just like me, they were wearing their regular practice jerseys.

"Are you guys on Gunnar's team?" I asked, edging past Kenny and the guys to catch up.

It would be cool to have a few of us Cougars on the team. And even better? If it was just Patrick, me and the benchwarmers, I'd be the star player, for sure.

"Nope," Curtis said, shaking his head.

"Me neither," Jeremy said. "But my sister is."

What?

I froze and Colin smashed into me, almost knocking me over.

"Geez, Nugget. What's your deal?" he asked, pushing past me.

I still couldn't move.

Jeremy's *sister* would be on my team?

Patrick had stopped when I did and he was giving me a questioning look. But I couldn't speak.

I'd been so busy worrying about being on Katie Gunnar's team, I hadn't thought about who my teammates could be, other than the Port Alberni guys.

I definitely hadn't considered the possibility of girls.

Seriously? Girls?

"Jeremy's *sister*?" I mumbled.

Patrick nodded. "Her name's Tonia, I think. She's on the —"

Before he could say another word, we were at the edge of the rink, where we could see the swarm of dark blue helmets on the far side of the ice. There were ponytails hanging out of some of them and curls sticking out of the others.

"Cutter Bay Blizzard," I finished for him, through gritted teeth.

Just when I thought things couldn't get any worse, I was going to be playing with a bunch of junior high girls who probably cared more about nail polish than pucks.

"There's Katie!" Patrick said, pointing to the far goal. "Come on, Nugget."

He grabbed my arm and pulled me onto the rink.

Even the familiar sound of my blades scraping the ice wasn't enough to make me feel better. Hockey had always been the highlight of my whole life, but I had the sinking feeling that was about to change.

Patrick let go of me and raced toward the girls' side.

I took my time following him and noticed that if I squinted, the Blizzard's blue helmets and jerseys looked like a dark cloud.

And I was going to be stuck in the middle of it.

I glanced toward the opposite net and saw the Cougars gathering around a guy who had to be Holbrook. He didn't look as big as he probably was, because Bosko, the gorilla, was standing right next to him.

Great.

They'd probably end up being best friends by the end of the week.

So Bosko and I shared right wing on the Cougars and we shared time with a Math textbook, but we wouldn't be sharing Danny Holbrook.

Nuts.

What if Bosko turned into an even better player than he already was? What if he started getting more game minutes than me?

It wasn't fair.

I looked at the rest of the guys on the other side of the rink and sighed.

Along with Bosko, Holbrook's team was made up of the rest of us Cougars, a couple of guys I didn't recognize and three girls.

They all wore Holbrook jerseys and it actually *hurt* to look at all of that blue and green, so I turned away to focus on my own team. I skated past centre ice, slowing down as I got closer to the dark cloud.

At least there were a few guys in the mix. Patrick was leaning on his stick and talking to Katie Gunnar while two of the Watson triplets passed a puck back and forth between them. I glanced back at Holbrook's team and saw the other Watson talking to Kenny. How did they get split up? When I turned back to our side, I saw the Cougars' third benchwarmer, Tim Shaw, sitting on our bench.

The last two guys on the bench were from Port Alberni and even though we'd played them a million times, I didn't know their names.

I was pretty sure that was about to change.

So, including me, we had seven guys and nine girls.

Which meant we were already outnumbered.

A whistle sounded and I turned to see that Katie Gunnar was the one blowing it.

"Come on over," she called, waving her glove in the air.

"Here goes nothing," I muttered, as I skated toward her team.

By the time me and the rest of the guys had joined them, the Blizzard's chatter had turned into giggling.

Lots of giggling.

One girl with a blond ponytail turned to look at me, then whispered to two of her teammates. They all started giggling even louder.

I glanced at the Watsons, who shrugged.

"What's so funny?" I asked.

"Who knows?" one said.

The girls looked at me again and giggled even louder.

I poked the blonde in the back with my stick and asked again, "What's so funny?"

She turned and grinned at me. "You're cute."

And they all shrieked with laughter.

"You've got to be kidding me," I muttered.

"I don't know, Nugget," the other Watson said. "Maybe you *are* cute, and you just never knew it."

"Very funny," I said, giving him a jab to the ribs with the butt of my stick.

"Wow. Cute *and* tough," he said, laughing.

"Okay, everybody, let's get started," Katie Gunnar said over the racket.

The girls all quieted down the second she took off her helmet. She had straight brown hair pulled back in a tight braid, and her face was covered with freckles. She wasn't wearing gobs of makeup, like I expected, but her smile was huge, like she was in the middle of a toothpaste commercial.

That smile was way over the top.

"I'm Katie Gunnar, and first off, I'd like to thank you all for signing up."

"I didn't," I mumbled to myself.

Patrick glanced over his shoulder at me. "Shh."

"This is going to be a fun week," Katie continued, "but it's also going to be a lot of hard work."

"Yeah, right," I whispered to Tim, who shot me a dirty look and turned back to the coach.

"As you probably know already, I'm a member of the Canadian Women's Hockey Team."

"Woo-hoo!" one of the girls called out and a couple of others cheered.

"Thank you," Katie said, laughing. "We've won gold medals at the last two Olympic Games and I have to tell you that those were two of the proudest moments of my life."

"Are you wearing your medals now?" one of the Blizzard asked.

Katie laughed. "No."

"I'd be wearing mine," she said.

"I hope you get the chance someday," she said, with an even bigger smile. "Now, let's go through my list and make sure everyone is here. Cara Vittoli?"

"Here," a redhead squeaked.

"Tonia Simpson?"

Jeremy's sister.

"Here," a female version of my buddy raised her hand.

As soon as Katie said my name, I raised my hand to let her know I was there and stopped listening. There had to be a way out of this mess.

I looked at Holbrook's team, lined up against the boards while he talked to them about the kind of stuff I could only imagine.

Man, I wished I was over there.

Especially when I saw him pull a cardboard box out onto the ice. He opened it up and let the guys dig into it. I saw Jeff pull out a handful of tuques, Kenny had a pennant and the rest of the guys were grabbing at either stickers or badges. I was too far away to tell.

I gritted my teeth, wishing I hadn't even looked, and tried to concentrate on what was happening at my end of the rink.

Katie Gunnar was still taking attendance.

I should have paid more attention, so I'd at least know the names of the Port Alberni guys, but I didn't really hear anything until she said, "Ashley Bosko."

I spun around and stared as a stick was waved in the air.

Ashley *Bosko*?

I knew Eddie had an older brother. After all, Shane was dating Wendy. But a sister? Ashley? I'd never heard of her. I glanced at Tim and Patrick, but neither of them was looking in my direction.

A whistle was blown on the other side of the rink and I watched the guys skate into their positions.

That's when I realized that the situation was even worse than I'd thought.

Bosko was spending time with Danny Holbrook while I was stuck with his *sister*.

The whole world had gone totally nuts.

Katie finished going through her list, then she slid a big cardboard box out from behind the net and tore it open.

"I have a little something for you guys," she said, digging inside.

I waited for her to start pulling out pink jerseys, my stomach in knots over the whole stinkin' mess.

To my total surprise, she didn't.

In fact, the jerseys weren't bad. They were mostly grey, with black sleeves and a bit of light blue here and there. The logo was a puck with blue wings, which was a bit too much like Detroit's logo for my taste, but pretty cool anyway.

I had to admit, I was impressed.

"I've got to tell you," Katie said, as she passed blond-ponytail a jersey, then gave one to little redhead. "I didn't realize you'd all be so big."

I couldn't help smiling. As the smallest eleven-year-old on my team, at school and probably on the entire planet, I'd never been called a big guy before.

I liked it.

"I ordered mostly mediums, so I'm not sure I have enough jerseys that will fit," she said, cringing.

What? I might not even get a jersey?

I looked over at the Holbrook team in their blue and green. It wasn't fair.

Nothing was fair.

I watched Katie hand out jerseys to the rest of the girls first, since most of them were bigger (well, taller) than us.

"I'm really sorry," she said to the rest of us, when she'd given a couple of the guys the last of the mediums.

I sighed.

"Jonathan?" Katie said.

"Yup."

"I think a small will work for you," she said, tossing me a jersey.

I felt my cheeks get warm and knew my face was bright red.

"Thanks a lot," I mumbled.

My heart sunk when I checked the tag. It was an extra small. And even worse? I knew it would fit.

Katie gave the rest of the guys their jerseys but it was pretty obvious the sizes were way off. When Patrick held his up against his body, it didn't look like it was long enough to reach his belly button.

So, only me and the Blizzard girls had the matching black and grey.

Just perfect.

"If you could wear those tomorrow, that would be great

and in the meantime I'll put in an express order for the guys."

For the guys?

If they were the guys, what was I supposed to be?

"So let's get this camp going," Katie said. "We'll warm up first by skating lines and —"

"You've got to be kidding," I muttered. We skated lines all the time at practice. Camp was supposed to be fun!

"Is there a problem, Jonathan?" Katie asked.

"No . . ." Of course there was. "Okay, it's already bad enough that we have a bunch of girls on the team and —"

"Bad enough?" Katie asked, one eyebrow raised.

"You know what I mean." I shrugged. "And this is supposed to be camp, not practice. I already know how to skate lines."

She tilted her head to one side, just like Mum did when she was getting mad.

Uh-oh.

"Then why don't you show the rest of us?" she said, with a smile that was cooler than the ice I stood on.

"By myself?" I asked.

"I'll do it too," the red-haired girl offered, then turned to look me over, from helmet to blades. "And crush you."

"What?" I had to hold back a laugh. She was the smallest girl there. "You mean race? You're like, half my size."

"Well, you're half the size of my brother," she said, giving me a cold stare. "And he's nine."

"Hey!" I gasped.

Katie blew her whistle. "That's enough chatter, I think. Are you ready, Jonathan?"

I nodded. I was ready, all right. Ready to leave my competition in the dust.

Half the size of a nine-year-old? *Come on.*

"Ready, Cara?"

The girl nodded, and the very second the whistle sounded, she took off like she'd been fired from a slingshot.

Caught off guard, I had a slower start, but I made sure I picked up speed right away.

All I could hear behind me were a couple of shouts of "Go, Nugget!" before the guys were completely drowned out by the frantic screams of nine girls. They sounded like the howling sirens of the Cutter Bay Fire Department.

Cara leaned over and touched the line with one gloved hand, then spun around to head back to the net, grinning and flashing a mouthful of braces as she passed me.

It was *on.*

I kicked it into high gear and bent to touch the ice myself. When I turned to head back, already breathing hard, I could see that the Cougars on Danny Holbrook's team had stopped what they were doing to watch.

Nuts.

I pushed myself even harder and started to catch up with Cara. By the time she touched and turned by the goal, I was only a couple of paces behind her. My lungs were on fire, but I was in it to win it.

I wasn't going to get smoked by some girl from the Blizzard.

Not in this lifetime.

A few of the Cougars were cheering for me while others were shaking their heads as I worked to catch up to that stupid blue helmet.

Cara and I hustled back and forth for what seemed like forever until Katie shouted "Last one!"

I couldn't believe it, but I actually had another burst of

speed left in me. I pushed myself as hard as I could, breathing hard through my mouth, nose and for all I knew, my ears.

I'm not sure if it was adrenalin or embarrassment, but I somehow managed to drag myself across the finish line first.

I won by less than a metre.

The guys on both sides of the rink cheered for me while I skated a victory lap.

As I returned to my goal, all nine members of the Blizzard lined up, arms folded across their chests, and glared at me like I'd cut in line at a Twilight movie.

That's when I knew it was a double win.

They didn't think I was cute anymore.

Chapter Four

I skated back to the guys and found a spot between Patrick and one of the Port Alberni players.

"That could have been embarrassing," the one with the big nose said.

"*Could* have been?" the skinny one asked, snorting.

"I won," I reminded them.

"Barely," Big Nose pointed out.

My lungs were killing me and it was taking everything I had to sound like I wasn't gasping for breath. The last thing I needed was an earful from those guys.

"Look, I had it under control, okay?" I told them, sounding a lot more sure than I felt.

"Sure, you did," Skinny said, sarcastically. "You almost bit it on that last turn."

He was right, but there was no way I'd admit it. "Not even close," I told him.

Patrick elbowed me in the ribs and I noticed that the whole team was silently staring at me and the Port Alberni guys.

"Am I keeping you from something?" Katie asked,

giving us a tough look. "Something maybe more important than hockey?"

"No," we all said quickly.

I heard a snort from down the line and when I checked to see who it was, Ashley Bosko was laughing at me.

Whatever.

I glared back and when I really looked at her, I saw that she didn't look like Bosko at all. Her hair was light brown instead of almost black, and she had blue eyes instead of dark brown. Of course, she didn't have Bosko's mustache (which he shouldn't have had, himself!) and she was normal sized instead of a giant.

Lucky for her.

"Okay," Katie said, interrupting my thoughts. "Now that Jonathan and Cara have shown us how it's done, let's all skate lines."

What?

I'd barely caught my breath and my legs were still burning. I cleared my throat. "Uh, Katie?"

"Gunnar," she said. "Everyone calls me Gunnar."

"Okay, Gunnar," I said, then added, "And everyone calls me Nugget." I pointed to myself and Cara. "Do we have to do it again?"

Another snort from Ashley Bosko.

I ignored her. Well, tried to, anyway.

"Are you already worn out?" Gunnar asked, with an innocent smile.

"Well . . ."

"I'm not," Cara said, skating to the goal line. "I'm ready for more."

"Nugget?" Gunnar said. "If you want to hit the bench for a rest —"

"No!" I interrupted. "No, I'm cool. Let's do this." I took a deep breath and prepared to blow everybody away with how hard I could work and how fast I could move.

Of course I didn't need a rest!

Especially if Cara didn't need one.

"Are you okay?" Patrick whispered from his spot beside me.

"I'm awesome," I lied, trying to make my breathing sound normal.

"You look kind of . . . exhausted."

"I'm fine," I told him.

"You know, the girls are all a year or two older than us."

"I know."

"They've been playing longer, Nugget."

"I *know*," I snapped, starting to get ticked off. I didn't need an excuse for losing to a girl because I *didn't* lose.

He shrugged. "I'm just saying."

Once we were all lined up, Gunnar blew her whistle and I took off like my life depended on it.

My blades cut the ice faster than they did the first time around. My legs felt heavy at first, but once I got into the skating rhythm, I didn't notice anymore.

I was seriously hustling and keeping up with everyone.

And that was a good thing, because it turned out that Cara the redhead wasn't the fastest girl out there. There were three Blizzards who were seriously smoking the rest of us.

And the guys from Port Alberni were hauling, too.

I bent to touch the line and spun around smoothly, then took off for our goal line again. My legs felt good, but everything else was struggling. I tried to keep my breathing nice and even, but my throat and lungs felt like they belonged to somebody else. Somebody who was ready to lie down for a while.

I gritted my teeth, thinking about the times I'd been put to the test, especially going up against Bosko. I knew I could pull out all the stops if I had to.

And to save face on first day of camp, I definitely had to.

There were a handful of kids ahead of me, but that was about to change. I took a deep breath and ignored the raw feeling in my lungs. I lifted my left skate before my right blade had even hit the ice. And I did the same with my right, then my left again, picking up speed.

I was going for it! Practically flying!

I pumped my arms as quickly as I could, passing Tim and two members of the Blizzard.

Yes!

I touched the line, pulled another smooth turn and started racing for the next one. Pretty soon, I was one of the frontrunners, keeping pace with Patrick, Skinny Port Alberni and a girl with two long, dark braids poking out from under her helmet.

Man, was she fast!

But, in the end, I was faster.

I crossed the goal line for the last time, ahead of everyone else. Even though my knees were shaking and my lungs were empty, I felt awesome.

"Good job," Patrick said, skating over and patting me on the back.

"You, too." I looked over at Danny Holbrook's camp and saw that they were split into two teams, busy scrimmaging.

As awesome as it felt to beat everyone at skating lines, I would have rather been *playing*.

"Those Holbrook jerseys are awesome," I said.

"Yeah, but seriously, Nugget, who would put their own name on every jersey?" He watched them with me, then whispered, like an announcer, "Holbrook passes to Holbrook, who loses the puck to Holbrook, but can he out-skate Holbrook? Holbrook's looking pretty nervous in goal, knowing that Holbrook has a heck of a slapshot."

"Very funny," I said, rolling my eyes.

I scanned the ice, looking for the Canuck. Other than seeing him huddled up with Bosko, I hadn't had a good look at the guy yet.

Where was he?

"Our team's over here," Tim reminded me.

"I know," I sighed. "It's just . . ."

"Danny Holbrook?" he finished for me.

"Yeah," I sighed.

Tim shrugged. "If you ask me, the dude's overrated."

"I didn't ask."

"Nice work on those lines, Nugget," Katie Gunnar said, suddenly appearing next to me. "You've got some stamina."

"And speed," I told her.

She laughed. "And a bit of an ego, maybe?"

"Definitely," Patrick said, nodding.

"Well, there's nothing wrong with knowing your strengths," Gunnar said, slapping me on the back.

"See?" I said, elbowing Patrick, who rolled his eyes.

"But it's important to be aware of your weaknesses, too," Gunnar added. Before I could say anything, she con-tinued, "Now let's get rolling, here."

And that's exactly what we did.

We spent the whole morning practising technical stuff, like skating backwards (a weakness of mine, I had to admit), changing directions in half a second, stick handling and, finally, shots on goal.

I glanced over at Holbrook's side to see if he was anywhere in sight. Part of me hoped he'd seen my magic on the ice and would demand that I switch to his team.

As I waited in line behind the rest of Gunnar's team, I imagined Danny Holbrook giving me a camp MVP award on Friday. I could practically feel the weight of a gigantic trophy in my arms.

"You're up, Nugget." Patrick said, poking me in the back.

"Cool," I said, taking the puck Tim passed me and skating toward the first orange cone.

It was a drill the Cougars did all the time, so weaving through the cones felt really smooth and natural.

What made it even better was that I was super warmed up after a whole morning of drills, so I felt nice and loose.

The goal was empty and I took my time lining up a shot that was guaranteed to impress Holbrook.

I swung my stick and connected with the puck perfectly. It whipped through the air and right into the top left corner of the net.

"Sweet," I whispered. What I really wanted to do was shake my fist in the air, like it was the winning shot in the last four seconds of the final Stanley Cup game. But I held back.

I passed Cara the puck and she took off toward the cones while I headed for the back of the line.

The whole way there, I expected to hear Holbrook's voice, asking who that awesome player was, but it didn't happen.

When I saw Cara's great shot, it got my attention and

from that point on, I almost forgot about Holbrook while I watched my own team.

After Cara's turn, a couple of other Blizzard girls showed that they had some skills, then Jeremy Simpson's sister Tonia took her shot and just nailed it. The puck moved so fast, I wished we had a radar gun to measure its speed.

Seriously.

Ashley Bosko was up next, and even though she had nothing on her brother, I had to admit she was decent, too.

The truth was, I was kind of impressed with most of the Blizzard girls. And maybe even kind of impressed with Katie Gunnar. She seemed to know what she was doing.

I looked over to Holbrook's side and saw him leaning against the penalty box while his guys went at it. Bosko had the puck and he was dodging defencemen like it was nothing. And to him, it was.

I heard Kenny shout that he was open, and Bosko passed to him.

While Danny Holbrook started digging around in his jacket pockets, I watched my best friend make the best shot of his life, scoring on Bedhead.

"Yes!" Kenny shouted.

"Nice play," I heard Bosko say while a couple of guys slapped Kenny on the back.

Holbrook didn't even look up, because he'd found what he was looking for.

A cell phone.

It probably means I'm a jerk, but I was kind of glad the coach had missed Kenny's shot. It would have stunk to watch a Canuck get all excited over Kenny's playing while I was stuck in Girlville.

I watched Colin shoulder-check Jeff, then pass the puck

to Chris. But Chris barely had it two seconds before Bosko stole it and headed for the goal.

I checked to see if Holbrook was watching, but he was too busy clearing his three girl players off the bench and into the penalty box so he could have a private phone conversation.

"Nugget, it's your turn," one of the Watsons said, passing me the puck.

I took off toward the cones, wondering who Danny Holbrook was talking to.

* * *

When both coaches blew their whistles, we all skated off the ice to grab our lunches from the locker room. My brown bag weighed a ton, but it was always hard to know whether that was good or bad. Heavy could mean something like a can of pop, but because Mum was a nutritionist, it could also mean a tub of hummus. And I knew from experience that it was impossible to explain hummus to the rest of the guys.

On my way back to the stands, I watched Gunnar walk over to Danny Holbrook with a big smile. She said something I couldn't hear and then her smile disappeared when he said only one or two words back and kept coming toward the stands.

Gunnar just stood there and watched him walk away for a few seconds, shaking her head, like she couldn't believe what she'd heard. Like he'd said something totally crazy.

Weird.

I was hoping Holbrook would come up into the stands and eat lunch with us guys. I figured it would be an awesome chance to hear some behind-the-scenes stories about the Canucks and what it was like to be a real NHL player.

Just because I wasn't on his team didn't mean I wouldn't be able to talk to the guy.

I actually started to feel kind of nervous about what to say to him. That is, until he turned left and headed for the main office.

Oh well, I had a whole six days to get to know him.

I kept climbing until I got to the rows that were loaded with most of the Cougars and sat down.

Just as I was opening my lunch bag, I noticed that Katie Gunnar was climbing the steps toward us.

Luckily, she joined the Blizzard girls, who were giggling and shrieking in their own group, a few rows down from the Port Alberni guys.

At least most of them were. Ashley Bosko was sitting a couple of rows up, kind of near the three girls from Holbrook's team, but not totally *with* them.

Whatever.

I dug into my bag, relieved when I saw that the heavy stuff was juice boxes.

"Trade you my mandarin for your brownie," Tim said to Patrick.

"No way."

"I'll take the mandarin," I told him. I loved those things and I'd already eaten the one from the toe of my Christmas stocking. "Want my fruit punch?"

"Deal."

I gave him the juice box, glad that Mum had packed three of them for me.

"So," Chris said, from his spot in front of me and Patrick. "How's it going?"

"Great," Patrick said.

"Seriously? he asked. "You *like* the girl's team?"

"Yeah." Patrick nodded.

"What are you guys gonna be called, anyway?" Colin asked. "If we're Holbrook's Heroes, who are you?"

"Gunnar's Girlies?" Jeff asked, through a mouthful of peanut butter and banana.

"You have girls on your team, too," I reminded him, getting annoyed.

"Only a couple, and not as our coach," Chris said. "You guys got burned."

"Totally burned," Kenny agreed.

I knew from experience that agreeing was what Kenny did best, so I didn't let it bug me.

"She's pretty cool, actually," one of the Watsons said, in between gulps of chocolate milk.

"Pretty cool," the second Watson repeated.

I waited for the third one to pitch in, but he was too busy with an awesome looking peanut butter cookie to get involved.

"Yeah well, she's not as cool as Holbrook," Chris said.

"Holbrook's not *that* cool," Patrick said.

Everyone stopped talking and even chewing to stare at him.

"Dude, he was a Canuck," Jeremy said.

"A long time ago," Patrick said, sounding pretty sure of himself.

"Yeah, well, Gretzky retired before I was even born," Chris said. "And I still think he's pretty cool."

"Obviously," Kenny said, and a couple of guys nodded.

"Hold on a second," Patrick said, waving a banana in the air. "Are you actually comparing Holbrook to Gretzky?"

"No, I'm just making a point."

"Do you know what that point is?" Patrick asked.

One of the Watsons snorted.

"Look," Chris sighed. "All I'm saying is I don't think you guys are getting your money's worth out of camp."

"What are you talking about?" Patrick asked.

"You didn't even get jerseys," Colin said.

"Yeah, we did," a Watson said. "We'll have them tomorrow."

"Are they in the shop?" Chris asked. "Having those last few sequins added?"

I knew we weren't going to get anywhere with that conversation.

"I saw all the hats and stuff Holbrook gave you guys," I said, kind of hoping somebody might offer to share.

"Pretty awesome," Jeff said, nodding.

"Was it all autographed?" I asked, thinking of how a few extra bits and pieces could round out my collection at home.

"No," Jeff said. "It wasn't Holbrook's stuff," he added, quietly.

"Was it signed by other Canucks?" Patrick asked.

"No," Bosko said. "The hats are from a burger place in Surrey, with their logo on them."

"Huh?" That didn't even make sense.

"The stickers were from —" Bosko began.

"A garage," Chris finished for him.

"Seriously?" I asked.

"And the calendars were from the Bank of Montreal."

"Hold on," I said. "None of it was hockey stuff?"

"No," Jeff said. "But it was free."

Man, if I was a retired pro, I would bring all kinds of cool stuff from my old team to hand out.

Bank calendars? Ugh.

What was Holbrook thinking?

Kenny piped in. "Who cares about whether the free stuff was any good?"

Judging by the looks on everyone's faces, we all did.

Kenny continued, "You guys have been doing drills and stuff all morning while we've been *playing*."

Bosko's deep voice came from behind me. "Drills are important."

Usually two or three words from Bosko were enough to shut everybody up. But not at hockey camp, I guess.

"Sure, at *practice*," Jeremy said. "But this is *camp*. The whole idea is to play."

I'm not sure what our number-one benchwarmer really knew about playing, but he did kind of have a point.

"Yeah," Kenny said. "I'm here to have fun."

"Me too," Chris said.

Maybe Chris was right and we really weren't getting our money's worth by running a thousand drills.

Maybe Katie Gunnar really *was* ripping us off.

Chapter Five

When I hit the ice again after lunch, I didn't want to waste any more time. Camp was only six days long, and the first day was already half over. Thanks to Eddie Bosko's tutoring, I could calculate that I had already wasted just over eight percent of my camp time on drills.

That meant we still had more than ninety percent left, and I was ready to make the best of it.

Gunnar blew her whistle and we all skated over to meet her at the goal line.

"I hope everyone is feeling full, happy and ready to work," she said, with another big smile. "We're going to work on fast turns this afternoon."

"Seriously?" I whispered to Patrick. "More drills?"

"I'm sure she has a plan," he whispered back.

It seemed to be about time I came up with one of my own.

I let everyone else get into line ahead of me and watched for a minute while pairs of players took a turn skating. When Gunnar blew her whistle, they had to change direction, turning right. The next time she blew it, they had to turn left. Every single time they heard the tweet, they had to switch. And Gunnar blew that whistle a *lot*.

Patrick and one of the Watson triplets were up, and they looked pretty good on the first couple of turns, but when Gunnar picked up the pace it turned into a bit of a mess.

Next was the other Watson and Tim, then Skinny and Big Nose from Port Alberni. Because there were only seven guys on the team, I was the odd one out, which meant I had to find a partner from the Blizzard.

"Fine," Ashley Bosko said, rolling her eyes.

"Fine what?"

"I'll do the drill with you."

"I didn't ask you to," I told her.

She leaned on her stick. "You were going to."

"Why don't you pair up with one of your friends?" I asked, pointing over my shoulder at the other girls.

"Too late," she said, with a shrug.

I turned to see that they were already split into twos. Great.

"Hey, why didn't all of you girls sit together at lunch?" I asked, hoping to distract her from wanting me for a partner.

She stared at me. "I don't know any of them."

"But you're the Blizzard," I reminded her. "You're a *team*."

"No, we're not," she said, shaking her head. "The girls on Holbrook's team are from Port Alberni."

Just like the extra guys on my team. What were they trying to do, take over Cutter Bay?

"Okay, so *they* aren't on the Blizzard but you're —"

"Not on any team this year."

"What? Why not?"

She sighed, like I should have known all of this stuff. "When we moved here in September, the Blizzard's roster was already full. I'll sign up for next season."

"But you're —"

"Trying to squeeze some hockey in during Christmas break, if you don't mind. So, are we partners?"

"It doesn't look like I have a choice." I sighed.

"Don't worry, Nugget," she said, with a laugh. "I won't embarrass you."

I stared at her. What was that supposed to mean? That she thought she could beat me at fast turns? Ha!

"I know you won't," I told her.

When it was our turn, I knew I did a better job than most of the kids, and I was definitely better than Ashley. She kept turning the wrong way and almost skating into me, no matter how many times I told her to watch out.

Of course, I'd done drills like that before. Dad got me to work on speed turns whenever we were on the ice together.

In other words, I was already getting Gunnar's training from him for free.

There really was no reason to pay for it.

I was hoping we'd at least squeeze in a scrimmage before the day was over, mostly because that was all Holbrook's team had done all stinkin' day.

But Gunnar had other ideas.

While she explained yet another drill, I decided I couldn't wait any longer. While Gunnar was setting up cones, I skated over to talk to her in private.

"What can I do for you, Nugget?" she asked, smiling.

I swear I'd never seen someone smile so much in my life. Like, ever.

I took a deep breath, knowing it was probably best to just get it over with, nice and fast.

"I think I should switch teams," I told her.

She tilted her head at me, like I was confused. "These are just drills. You're split into two lines, but they aren't *teams*."

"No. I mean, I think I should switch to Danny Holbrook's team," I told her.

She frowned. "Danny Holbrook's team," she repeated.

"It would be for the best." It was something Grandpa Charlie always said and I liked how it sounded.

She frowned even more. "The best for who?"

Me, obviously. But I couldn't say that.

"For . . . everyone." I shrugged.

"Go ahead and start, you guys," she called to the players who were waiting.

Instead of saying something, she watched Patrick and Cara work their way through the cones for a few seconds and shouted, "Nice work!"

I waited, but nothing was happening. I knew she'd heard me, because she'd repeated what I'd said. And it wasn't exactly a complicated idea that needed a lot of thought.

"I'd rather be playing, you know?"

She nodded, but didn't look at me. "Hmm."

Maybe I wasn't explaining myself the right way.

I took another try at it. "I mean, drills are cool and everything, but we do those all season, anyway."

She was quietly watching my teammates.

I cleared my throat. Maybe if she knew how simple the switch would be, that would convince her. "All you'd have to do is swap me for one of the girls. Easy."

She blew her whistle for the next pair to start and I saw Ashley line up next to one of the Watsons.

Part of me wondered whether I should just let it go for now and wait until the end of the day to talk to Gunnar.

The other part of me wasn't ready to give up, not if I could have a Holbrook jersey and play with the rest of the Cougars. The second part won.

"A lot of my teammates are on Holbrook's team and —"

"And a couple of them are on mine," she finally said.

"Yeah, five of us, but —"

She looked me in the eye for a second or two. "I think you should stay where you are."

"What? Why?" Couldn't she tell I was a way better fit for Holbrook's team?

She looked back at the players. "For today, anyway."

"So, I can switch tomorrow?" I asked, hopefully.

I could see her jaw tighten. "We can talk about it tomorrow."

"Do you mean talk to Holbrook? Talk to him and make the switch?"

It wasn't exactly what I wanted, but at least I'd still have five whole days on Holbrook's team. And five days was plenty of time to show him what I could do. In five days, he'd make me MVP of the camp, for sure.

I could feel the weight of that trophy in my arms again. Would it be gold? Silver?

"No," Gunnar said.

"No what?" I asked.

"No, we aren't talking to Holbrook. Tomorrow *you and I* can talk more about you wanting to switch."

"We can do that right now," I told her.

"No, we can't. In case you haven't noticed, I'm in the middle of coaching a hockey camp."

"But if we —"

"The subject is closed until tomorrow," she said, and I could tell she meant it.

"Fine," I sighed.

"In the meantime, your footwork could use some improvement."

What?

"My foot—" I started to argue, but had the feeling it would be better to keep my mouth shut. All I had to do was get through the afternoon, then I'd have all night to come up with the perfect argument to convince her to trade me.

Gunnar tilted her head toward the cones. "Jump in."

When I skated back over to the team, I couldn't help noticing that Holbrook's guys were *still* scrimmaging, laughing and shouting like they were having the best time ever.

And they probably were.

Except the three girls in the penalty box, maybe.

They looked bored out of their minds.

"What's going on?" Patrick asked when I got in line behind him.

"I asked to switch to Holbrook's team."

"What?" Tim asked.

"I want to play, you guys."

"We are playing," Tim said.

"We're running drills," I told him, rolling my eyes. "This is Christmas break. We're supposed to be having fun."

"Not just having fun," Patrick said. "We're supposed to be improving our skills."

"Learning new things," one of the Watsons said.

Why didn't they care that we weren't getting our money's worth?

The answer hit me almost instantly.

They *were* getting their money's worth.

They needed the drills.

"I don't need to learn anything," I told him. And it was true. I was the best player out of the five of us.

It all made sense.

"Sure you do," Patrick said.

"What?" I practically choked.

"Not just you, Nugget," he said, patting me on the back. "I meant that we all do."

"The fast turns are good training," a Watson said.

"So are the cones," his brother added.

Didn't they get it? Not only was I a better player, but my main competition, Eddie Bosko, was about to become a total superstar with the help of a pro while I skated lines and played pass the puck with a bunch of girls.

All of the other Cougars were going to be better players by the end of the week. Never mind the fact that they'd be a tighter team and the five of us would be left behind.

"Look," I snapped. "I don't want to be on this team, okay?"

"Oh, man up, would ya?" a familiar voice said from her spot in the other line.

I turned to stare at Ashley Bosko. "What's that supposed to mean?"

"I think it's pretty obvious. Quit whining."

"I'm not whining," I said. Even to me, it sounded pretty whiny.

"Really?" she asked, leaning on her stick. "I'd give that one a nine out of ten."

She might not have looked like a Bosko, but she sure sounded like one.

"You don't understand," I told her, shaking my head.

"Not at all," she agreed.

I pointed at the sea of green and blue on the other side of the rink. "That's *my* team."

"Not this week," she said with a shrug. Then she turned away.

"She's right, you know," Tim said.

"Whatever," I sighed. "You're a benchwarmer."

"Excuse me?" he said, skating a little closer.

"You heard me. You're not exactly a hockey expert, you know?"

"At least I'm not a freakin' Timbit on skates," he snapped.

I heard Ashley Bosko snort again.

"Say that again," I told him. I dare you."

"Cut it out!" Patrick shouted.

I took a step back from him, totally surprised.

"He started it," Tim said, pointing at me.

"Who cares?" Patrick asked. "Just let it go, you guys."

Gunnar skated over to us. "*Another* problem over here?" she asked, raising an eyebrow at me.

"No," I said, looking anywhere but at her.

"I hope not," she said, skating in a slow circle. "I'd sure hate to have to kick anybody out of camp for bad behaviour."

What?

"I didn't even —"

"Or a bad attitude," she said over her shoulder as she skated back toward the goal line.

Kick someone out of camp for a bad attitude?

Come on.

"That's just great," I muttered.

"Can't you just get over yourself, Nugget?" Patrick asked. "Just enjoy the stupid camp?"

I felt bad as I watched him skate to the other line. I wasn't trying to ruin anything for Patrick. He was one of my favourite teammates and a good friend.

But I didn't have the energy to get into all of that.

I needed to focus all of my attention on figuring out how to convince Gunnar to trade me in the morning.

There had to be a way.

Since she'd mentioned kicking people out of the camp, I didn't want to do anything that would turn her against me (any more than she already was, anyway), so I worked really hard for the rest of the day. I took all of the drills seriously, pushing myself to do my best.

As a result, my speed was awesome, my stick handling was solid and when we worked on shooting, I nailed my first shot.

Of course, the goal was empty, so that was easy to do.

While I waited at the back of the line for my turn, I thought about the shot I'd taken from centre ice during halftime at the Canucks game a couple of months ago. I'd won the chance by playing a trivia game on PUCK radio.

That shot was on an empty goal, too. In front of thousands of people. And I'd missed it.

My hero, Jean Ducette, had made me feel okay about the whole mess, but I still wanted to be able to wow a pro.

And hockey camp seemed like the only time that could happen.

Cutter Bay wasn't exactly packed with NHL players. The Sedin twins weren't going to be sitting in at my next

Cougars practice. Luongo wasn't going to cruise down Daffodil Drive and catch my killer street hockey moves any time soon.

Nope. Danny Holbrook was my only chance.

I watched Bosko make a breakaway, shouldering Colin out of the way and totally outskating Chris and Jeff. More than anything, I wished it was me over there. Even though Bosko played it pretty cool, I knew he loved to play, and as he geared up for the shot on Bedhead, I knew his heart was pounding in his chest, just like mine did. And even if he didn't grin and shout when he scored (like me), I knew he'd be happy when he did.

I held my breath as Bosko got into position and swung his stick. I watched when it connected and the puck flew toward Bedhead. I heard the shouts of my Cougar teammates and the cheers of the rest of the Heroes as the black bullet whipped through the air and sailed past Bedhead's glove.

It was an awesome shot!

Man, I was jealous.

I looked for Danny Holbrook to see what he thought of the play, but I couldn't spot him anywhere.

Again.

I took a closer look at all of the players, then figured he was probably in the washroom or something. Even pros had to go sometimes.

Then, when I was turning back to my drill, I spotted him. He was sitting on the Visitors' bench, talking on his cell phone.

I imagined that on the other end of the call was his agent, or maybe one of the guys he used to play with. What if he was talking to Trevor Linden? How cool would that be?

I was up next. I glanced at Katie Gunnar and saw that she was watching Danny Holbrook too. But she was frowning.

Patrick Chen passed me the puck and I took off toward the cones, figuring Gunnar was probably just jealous that *she* wasn't the one talking to Linden.

Chapter Six

At dinner that night, Mum tried to load me up with a huge pile of asparagus. And I mean huge, like it would have totally covered my plate and half my placemat.

"No, thank you," I told her, hoping the combination of good manners and a big smile would stop her.

It didn't.

She held the scoop in mid-air. "How many servings of vegetables have you had today, Jonathan?" she asked.

Sometimes it totally stunk to have a nutritionist for a mother. If it was up to her, instead of a regular house, we'd be living in a food pyramid.

"Five?" I lied. Unfortunately, my answer sounded too much like a question.

"Name them," Wendy said, an evil gleam in her eyes.

I had to think fast. "Uh . . . carrots, celery and —"

"Carrots and celery?" Mum asked.

"Yup."

"Funny. I didn't pack either of those in your lunch."

Nuts!

"Oh. I, uh . . . traded one of the guys."

"What did you trade him so you could get your hands on some irresistible carrots?" Wendy asked, with a smirk.

I tried to think of what Mum had packed in that stupid brown bag. "One of my juice boxes."

"For veggies?" Wendy asked. "Yeah, right."

"Just eat the asparagus," Mum said, moving the scoop toward my plate.

I had to do something. There was no way I could eat all of it.

"How about three spears?" I asked Mum.

"Eight," she said.

"Five," I countered.

"Six, and that's my final offer."

Once my plate was contaminated with my most hated vegetable (next to eggplant), Dad passed me a piece of salmon. "How was camp, Nugget?"

"Okay, I guess."

He gave me a surprised look. "You *guess*? You were there, right?"

"Yeah, but you know. I was on the wrong team and everything." I couldn't help sighing.

"Wow," Wendy said, lifting her glass of milk like she was making a toast. "Pretty serious stuff, Nugget. That sounds like it could be the plot of an *awesome* TV movie."

"Very funny," I said, chewing on my salmon.

"Or maybe even a series," she said. "I never knew being eleven was *so* dramatic."

"Honey," Mum said, resting a hand on top of my sister's. "You were a lot more dramatic than this at eleven."

"Yeah, right," Wendy said.

"You don't remember the case of the bad perm?"

"It *was* a bad perm," Wendy snapped.

"Whoa," I said, surprised by the fast reaction.

"It was right before picture day, okay, troll?" she said, glaring at me.

"Calm down," I said, smiling.

"No," she growled. "It was the worst perm *ever* and I had no time to fix it."

"I think I've made my point," Mum said. I could tell she was trying not to laugh.

"Moving on," Dad said, turning to me before Wendy could get even more wound up. "What did you think of the coach?"

I shrugged. "She was okay."

"Nice?" Mum asked, hopefully.

"I guess." I ate a piece of the salmon, trying to put off the moment I had to put that stinkin' asparagus in my mouth.

"Well, that's good," Mum said.

She didn't understand at all.

"Nice is great for a school nurse," I explained. "But it isn't exactly what I was looking for in a hockey coach."

"Well, I'm sure you'll learn a lot from her," Dad said.

"Probably not," I said.

"How do you know?" Mum asked.

"Because I asked to switch teams."

The whole table went quiet.

"Wow. Totally rude, Nugget," Wendy said.

I shoved some asparagus in my mouth. "I wasn't trying to be rude."

Wendy shook her head. "Well, you're talking with your mouth full right now, so rude obviously comes naturally to you."

"Please finish chewing, Jonathan," Mum warned.

"What did she say?" Dad asked. "Katie Gunnar, I mean."

I swallowed the asparagus and gulped some milk, hoping to wash at least some of the grossness away. "She said we'd talk about it in the morning."

"Oh dear," Mum sighed. "You probably hurt her feelings."

I groaned. "This isn't about feelings."

As I said the words, I remembered how Gunnar had looked when she saw Danny Holbrook talking on the phone.

Jealous.

And if she was *hurt* by me asking to swap teams, too, I knew one thing for sure; Katie Gunnar was going to have to toughen up.

It was hockey, for crying out loud.

* * *

That night, Kenny showed up on my doorstep, his stick in his hand and an excited look on his face.

"What's going on?" I asked.

"They're doing construction on Tulip Lane."

"So?"

"So, they left all their equipment there overnight." He wiggled his eyebrows. "With security lights."

It only took half a second to figure out why he was excited. "Night hockey," I said, starting to smile.

"Yup. Are you in?"

I checked with Mum and Dad, who said it was fine as long as I was home by eight o'clock. That gave me an hour and a half to pound the pavement.

Awesome!

I was geared up and out the door in about three minutes flat.

"You're not wearing your Gunnar jersey?" Kenny asked, chuckling.

"Nope," I said, closing the door behind me.

"You know, I wasn't sure if you'd be home tonight. I thought you might be hanging out with the girls, playing Barbies or something."

I stopped and glared at him. "You really want to go there?"

He bit his lip. "Uh, no. I was just kidding, Nugget."

"Well, don't."

It took about five minutes to get to Tulip, and I was over it by then.

"Are we cool?" he asked, as we walked toward the other guys.

"Yeah," I said, nodding. "I just want this whole mess to be over with. I'm probably switching to your team tomorrow."

"Awesome!" he said, giving me a high five.

And it would be awesome.

The guys were warming up in their Holbrook jerseys, but I didn't mind.

I'd be wearing one too, in about twelve hours. I couldn't wait to pull on that green and blue jersey and learn from a pro.

Before we split into teams, I listened to the guys talking about how cool Holbrook was.

"I saw him on the phone while you guys were playing," I said. "Who was he talking to?"

Chris shrugged. "I don't know. He said it was an important call."

"I bet it was another player," I said.

"Probably." Chris smiled. "Or maybe it was someone from TSN, interviewing him."

I know I wasn't the only guy who started daydreaming when we heard that. How awesome would it be to have TV guys calling to ask me questions about *my* pro career?

Seriously awesome.

"Are we gonna play, or what?" Bedhead asked.

"Yeah," Patrick said. "Let's do this."

"I'll take Nugget," Colin said, and I tried to play it cool as I walked over to stand next to him.

I loved being the first guy picked!

"I'll take Patrick," Chris said.

"Kenny," Colin said.

"*That* Watson," Chris said, pointing.

"Me?" one of the triplets asked, frowning. "We have names, you know."

"Yeah, of course I know that," Chris said.

The Watson crossed his arms over his chest. "Then what are they?"

"Warren, Quinn and Simon."

"Very good. Which one am I?"

Uh-oh.

I didn't think a single one of us could tell them apart.

Chris licked his lips and glanced from one brother to the next and the next and back again. "Warren," he said.

All three Watsons shook their heads.

I had the feeling this conversation had been coming for a long time. Suddenly, I felt awful that I'd been lumping them all together forever.

But they were seriously *identical*. And they even dressed the same!

"Quinn?" Chris asked, hopefully.

Three more head shakes.

I think every guy there was glad he wasn't the one being asked.

"Simon," Chris said, with a nod, like he'd known all along. "Okay, I pick you, Simon."

It was Colin's turn to choose and he obviously didn't want to get caught up in the confusion because instead of making the smart choice (either Quinn or Warren Watson) he picked Tim (a benchwarmer).

Great.

Tim gave me a dirty look when he joined our side, and I kind of wished I hadn't said anything about the bench-warming at camp.

"Nugget," he said, with a quick nod.

"Hey," I said, nodding back and hoping things weren't going to get awkward.

It stunk that since I'd joined Gunnar's team, hockey was suddenly more about feelings than faceoffs.

Once the rest of the guys had been picked for teams, I could forget about all of that. All of the Cougars were ready for action.

It was game time!

I got into position, and when Jeff took possession of the orange ball, he passed it right to me.

I took off like I was on fire, making my way toward the goal.

"Shoot!" Colin shouted.

But I wasn't ready. I knew from experience how impor-tant it was to line up the shot just how I wanted it. I kept tight control of the ball, so when Patrick came after it, he didn't stand a chance.

"Shoot!" Colin shouted again.

This time, I did.

I swung the stick and knew the shot was golden as soon as it hit the air.

Bedhead lunged for it, but tripped. He ended up skidding across the pavement on one elbow and the side of his face.

That was the tricky part about street hockey: no gear.

All of us gasped at once, like we were sucking all the oxygen out of Cutter Bay. When he stopped sliding, a few of us ran over to make sure he was okay.

I gritted my teeth when I saw the bumpy road rash that was already turning his cheek red. About forty percent of my body knew how that felt.

"Are you all right?" Kenny asked.

Bedhead looked a bit shocked, but when he touched his face and didn't see any blood on his fingers, he nodded.

"Yeah, shake it off," Colin said, when Bedhead got back on his feet.

"You still wanna play?" Jeff asked.

Bedhead stared at him like he was crazy. "Are you kidding me?"

We all laughed with relief.

"So, it's one–zip," I said, ready for more.

It felt good to be out there with the rest of the guys, all playing together on pavement instead of split up on the ice.

My team turned out to be a pretty good combination of players and I was surprised to see that Tim was actually better than I'd thought.

"I'm open," I shouted, when I saw him struggling to keep possession of the ball.

He pressed one foot on the ball while he turned around. He gave it a quick tap with his shoe to get it away from Patrick's stick, then passed it to me.

Chris was on me right away, scraping his stick against the pavement as he dug at the ball.

But I wasn't going to give it up. I twisted so my back was facing him, blocking his way.

"Shoot, Nugget!" somebody yelled.

I didn't have a clear shot, so I looked for somewhere to pass. Kenny was barely being covered by maybe Warren Watson, so I flicked the ball over to him.

Kenny took off with it, dodging past another Watson (Simon?) and finding an opening. He licked his lips and sized up the shot.

Bedhead braced himself for it.

He didn't need to, though, because Kenny fired it way over the net and past the lights. The last I saw of the ball was a flicker of orange as it disappeared into the darkest, deepest bunch of trees ever.

We'd never find it.

"Great," I sighed.

"Nice one, Cavanaugh," Chris groaned.

"Does anybody have another ball at home?" Jeff asked.

Most of the guys shook their heads while Tim mentioned something about a basketball, like that would help.

"I guess the game's over," Patrick said, shaking his head.

He was right, of course. We'd tried to play without a ball before, but rocks, pine cones and rolled-up socks just didn't do the job.

I stared into the trees, wondering if Canadian Tire could order some glow-in-the-dark balls.

Night hockey was awesome, but it definitely had some drawbacks.

* * *

The next morning, my alarm went off and I hit the snooze button but didn't fall asleep again. Instead, I stretched a bit, feeling how sore my muscles were from Gunnar's drills. Sore in a good way, though.

When I was finished, I lay there for a couple of minutes, trying to think of what I would say to her when I got to the rink.

She'd kind of shot down the idea that I didn't need more drills when she said my footwork could use some improvement. (My head was still spinning a bit over that one. Had she *seen* me skate?)

She probably wouldn't understand that I wanted to play with my friends, either, especially with four other Cougars on her team already.

How was I going to convince her to let me switch?

I sighed as I rolled out of bed and headed for the shower.

I was relieved to see that Mum had stocked up on guy shampoo and my Tuesday was off to a better start than Monday.

That is, until I tried to lather up my hair with shampoo and yelped with pain. Man, I thought my legs were sore, but they had nothing on my shoulders! Which one of Gunnar's drills was making me feel like I'd spent all day lifting Mum's minivan over my head?

Hockey was about being tough, so I pushed through the shampooing as fast as I could.

After my shower, I dressed in my sweats and went downstairs to pull the grey Gunnar jersey out of my hockey bag.

When I held it up, I realized it was actually cooler than Holbrook's. I'd been so focused on staring at the green and blue across the ice, I'd never really looked at hers again.

"What's that?" Mum asked, from the doorway to the mudroom.

I held the jersey up so she could see the front.

With the wings on either side of the puck, the logo didn't really look as much like Detroit's as I'd thought. The blue and black helped, too.

"Great design," Mum said. "I love it."

I was surprised to realize I did, too.

"I don't need it, since I'll be on the other team," I said, dropping it on the little bench over the heater and re-packing my old Canucks one.

"But someone else will, won't they?"

I hadn't thought about that.

"Yeah. Whoever switches with me, I guess," I said, nodding.

Whichever girl replaced me would probably be pretty happy to get out of Holbrook's penalty box for a change. Sure, she'd be stuck doing drills with Gunnar, but at least she'd be out on the ice.

I shoved the jersey back into the bag.

The truth was, now that I'd really looked at it, I kind of wanted to keep it for myself.

Chapter Seven

Mum dropped me off at camp with a lunch I had the sinking feeling was way overloaded with vegetables.

On my way into the rink, I saw that Ashley Bosko was already going through the front door, but Eddie was lagging behind.

"Hey, Bosko," I called out, then caught up to him.

He nodded to me. "How's it going, Nugget?"

"Good," I told him. "I'm being traded."

I loved the sound of that. It was like a pre-season deal in the NHL.

"You're what?" he asked, in a way that kind of ruined the moment.

"I'm switching to Holbrook's team today."

He turned to look at me, his thick eyebrows bunched together, like he was confused. And Bosko was never confused. "Seriously?"

I stared right back. "Uh, yeah."

"Why?"

What did he mean, why?

"Holbrook," I said, shrugging.

"What about him?"

I reached for the front door and pulled it open. As I walked through, I reminded him, "The guy was a *Canuck*, Bosko."

"And?" he asked, following me through the door.

"I'd rather learn from the best."

Bosko laughed. "Okay, NHL players are only the best in North America."

"Only?" I gasped.

"Let me finish," he said, holding up one massive hand to stop me. "Gold medalists are the best in the world." He paused. "Gunnar was on the team that was the *best in the world.*"

"Twice," I said, quietly.

"Right. So even if Holbrook had won a Stanley Cup —"

"He didn't." No one to remind me that the Canucks never had. That was the most painful part of being a fan. I could never forget.

"Even if he *had*, the Olympics are a whole other level."

I sighed. "I get what you're saying. It's just that I'd rather be on Holbrook's team."

Bosko shrugged. "My sister says Gunnar's a pretty good coach."

"I guess," I said. "But, you know."

"What? That she's a . . . she?" he asked.

"Well, yeah."

"You really can't get past that?" he asked, chuckling. "Your own sister is the best volleyball player I've ever seen."

"You watch volleyball?" I asked, snorting.

Bosko elbowed me a little harder than he needed to. "Wendy's beautiful —"

I almost puked right there.

"— and a great athlete," he finished.

"Your sister isn't bad, either."

Before I even knew what was happening, Bosko had my feet off the ground as he pinned me to the wall.

"What did you say?"

"Your sister," I choked, feeling totally panicked. It was my worst Bosko nightmare come to life (and probably death, for me!). "She's a good *athlete*. A good hockey player."

He stared me in the eye for a few seconds, then let me go. I slid down the wall and when I was standing again, I tried to make my knees stop shaking.

"Yeah," he finally said. "She's not bad."

"Exactly." I nodded, trying to catch my breath. Total terror had wiped me out.

"But don't mess with her," he warned.

My heart sped up again. "What do you mean, mess with her?"

"No playing rough out there, Nugget."

"I wouldn't. Not with a girl, anyway. And I'm not even going to be on her team after this morning."

He didn't seem to be listening.

"If she gets hurt, I'm holding you responsible."

"What?" I gasped.

"You heard me."

I pictured the girl who'd told me to man up and bossed me around on the ice.

"She's not going to get hurt," I told him. "You don't have anything to worry about. She's kind of a thug."

Bosko's nostrils flared as he took a step closer to me. "Did you just call my sister a *thug*?"

What?

I couldn't say she was beautiful (not that I wanted to — gross!), *or* that she was tough? What did the guy want from me?

I took a deep breath. "All I'm saying is she seems like she can take care of herself."

"But she won't have to," Bosko said, poking me in the chest with a thick finger. "Because you will. Right?"

It was another one of those rhetorical questions that didn't need an answer. Mostly because it *wasn't* a question. It was a threat.

I nodded and followed him into the rink, wishing I'd kept my stupid mouth shut.

* * *

I walked into the locker room and dropped my bag on the floor so I could start unpacking my gear. While I unzipped my bag, I listened to Kenny tell a joke I'd heard a hundred times before. By the time I'd pulled out my Canucks jersey, three different guys had shouted out the punch line.

"Why'd you guys have to wreck it?" he asked, pulling his Holbrook jersey over his Red Wings shirt.

"Because you keep telling it," Chris said.

"Because it's *funny*," Kenny said.

"Only the first time," Jeff told him.

I didn't really talk to anybody while I was getting my gear on, mostly because I was hurrying to get out to the office to talk to Gunnar before we got started for the day.

I'd taped my stick on Christmas Day, but after all of the work Gunnar had us do on day one, it was already looking kind of messed up.

And speaking of messed up, I'd felt okay when I'd stretched at home, and I'd thought the shower had finished the soreness off, but once I got out of the car, my muscles had really started to ache. Suddenly, my whole body was stiff, like I'd done a triathlon instead of one day of holiday camp.

"Are you sore, too?" Patrick asked, wincing as he lifted his helmet onto his head.

"Yeah," I told him, surprised.

"She really worked us out."

"Seriously?" Chris asked, looking up from the skates he was lacing.

"Yeah," Tim said, bending to stretch his back out, then his legs. "It feels good, though."

He was right about that. I knew from years of playing hockey that there was nothing like the stiffness of muscles and the crack of bones to make you feel like you'd really done something out on the ice.

Once I was dressed, I laced my skates and pulled the Gunnar jersey out of my bag so I could turn it in.

"Are you gonna wear two at once?" Colin asked. "Or wave one like a flag?"

"It's for my replacement," I told him. "I'm switching teams."

"She's letting you?" one of the Watsons asked. "I wouldn't mind switching too."

"I thought you liked her," I said, surprised.

"I do. I mean, she's a good coach and everything, but what if Holbrook's better?"

"What?" I asked. Where was this guy when I needed backup? "This is like, the opposite of what you were saying yesterday."

He frowned. "I didn't say anything about her yesterday."

"That was *me*," another Watson said.

"Which one *are* you?" I finally asked, and the whole locker room went quiet, like I shouldn't have.

But none of us knew! Somebody *had to* ask.

"Which *what* am I?" he asked.

"Which Watson?" I decided that honesty was probably the best move. "We can't tell you apart."

"Speak for yourself," Chris said, even though he'd already proven he was as stumped as the rest of us.

"We're totally different people," another Watson said

"Sure, but —" I began.

"His favourite colour is blue," the first Watson said, pointing to his brother. "And mine is orange."

"Seriously?" Kenny asked. "Why *orange*?"

Totally not the point. "Favourite colours don't help," I interrupted.

"Okay, well, he's allergic to strawberries," the third Watson said, pointing at the second.

"That *also* doesn't help us tell you apart," I groaned.

"It would if we were eating strawberries," the third one argued.

"Yeah, my face would be all puffed up," the second one said.

"You guys —"

"I'm Simon, he's Warren and he's Quinn," one snapped, tilting his head at both brothers as he named them. "Anyway, the point is, I wouldn't mind switching teams, too. It might be pretty cool."

"Yeah," Tim said. "Holbrook would be funner than Gunnar."

"Good one," Warren said, high-fiving him.

"Sure, if funner was actually a word," Patrick said. "It would be *more fun* to be on Holbrook's team."

"I think so, too," I nodded.

Patrick spun around to scowl at me. "I don't mean *I* think it would be more fun."

"Well, four of us do," I told him.

"Three, actually," Quinn said. "I think I'll stay where I am."

"You're changing your mind?"

He frowned. "*I* never said I wanted to switch."

I gave up on ever being able to tell them apart.

"Okay," I said, doing the math. "It just so happens that there are three girls on Holbrook's team who can be traded."

It would be way easier for three guys to convince Gunnar than just me. And three girls for three guys would be the easiest trade ever.

"Perfect," Tim said, smiling.

"Totally perfect," I agreed, thinking it was pretty cool that all of the girls on Holbrook's team would get out of the penalty box, too.

It was a win-win.

Or a win-win-win, actually.

Patrick just shook his head. "I'm telling you guys, Gunnar knows what she's doing."

"So do we," I told him, leading Tim and the trading Watson out toward the rink.

When I spotted Gunnar by the front office, I thought they were still following me, but when I turned around, I was alone.

"Gunnar?" I said.

"Hey, Nugget." She smiled until she saw the jersey in my hand. "Oh."

"I brought this in for whoever is taking my place."

"Is that right?" she asked.

"Yeah. There are a couple of other guys who want to switch, too," I told her. "So I figured three guys for three girls would be pretty easy."

"Three of you," she said, nodding slowly.

"Yeah. Me, Tim and, uh . . . Simon." I was pretty sure that was the right triplet.

"We were going to discuss the subject this morning."

"I know. That's why I came looking for you. So we can get it all taken care of."

She shook her head. "There was no decision made, Nugget."

"What do you mean?"

She looked at me for a long time without saying anything, then finally sighed and said, "I'm sorry."

"For what?" I asked.

"You can't switch."

"What?" I gasped. "Says who?"

"Says *me*," she said.

"What? Why can't —"

"I think you guys need to stay right where you are."

"For today?" I asked, hopefully.

"For camp."

"All week?" I asked, through the lump in my throat.

"Yes."

"But that's not fair."

She shrugged. "You'll just have to deal with it."

"But I —"

"*Deal with it,*" she said again, and I could tell by her tone that the conversation was over.

I couldn't believe it!

She'd said we were going to talk about it, but she'd just

said no, without even giving me a reason. It totally wasn't fair!

The Gunnar jersey was still in my hand when I walked back over to the guys. They could tell by the look on my face that my plan had gone down the tubes.

"What happened?" Simon asked, looking worried.

"She won't let us switch," I muttered.

"Why not?" Tim asked.

I shrugged and walked back to the locker room, where I balled up the jersey and shoved it deep into my bag. I might be stuck on Gunnar's team, but I didn't have to broadcast it.

And I didn't have to like it, either.

So I didn't.

When Gunnar welcomed us to day two of camp, I didn't even look at her. When she had us skate some laps to warm up, I took my time. I wasn't going to knock myself out to impress her.

"Maybe you should get moving," Patrick said, lapping me.

"I don't think so," I said.

"This is no different than when your Dad took over for Coach O'Neal and the guys gave him attitude."

"This is totally different."

"No, Nugget. You're acting like my two-year-old brother."

"If you're trying to call me a baby, just do it," I snapped, knowing he wouldn't.

On the way by, he said, quietly enough that no one but me would hear, "You're being a baby."

I ignored him.

Well, tried to, anyway.

I slowed down a little more to watch Holbrook's team

get started on their day. Of course, they'd be scrimmaging. Again.

I watched Bosko passing the puck back and forth with Colin, then saw Chris and Jeff warming up by taking shots on the empty goal.

Nobody was doing drills.

Nobody but us.

While everyone on my team lapped me a second time, I saw Gunnar head over to Danny Holbrook. I stopped skating completely, hoping she had changed her mind and was telling him about the switch.

I watched closely as she talked for about a minute, pointing to the girls in the penalty box a couple of times. That was a good sign. She was moving her hands around and seemed to have a lot to say.

Holbrook's Heroes, here I come!

But when she finished talking, Holbrook shook his head. I was no lip reader, but the word "no" was pretty obvious.

Come on!

I watched Gunnar head back over to our team, looking kind of ticked off. It was probably because she was the one hearing a big "no" this time.

"Now you know how it feels," I muttered.

"Are you talking to me?" Ashley Bosko asked.

"No."

She looked over each of her shoulders and saw no one else. "So you're talking to yourself."

"Maybe," I said, annoyed.

I looked at the Heroes and saw that Bosko was watching me. Ashley was going to get me killed, for sure.

"You gonna pick up the pace?" she asked.

"Why do you care?" I asked.

"Because you're really slow and it's a drag to have to keep skating around you. This isn't an obstacle course, you know."

I moved to the side so she could pass more easily.

"You're seriously not going to speed up?"

I shook my head. "Nope."

"Geez, why are you even here?"

It was a good question, one I couldn't stop asking myself for the rest of the laps. In fact, I ended up concentrating so hard on looking for an answer, I didn't even notice when I started to skate a little faster, then a little faster than that, until I was the one lapping my teammates.

I wish I could say that all of my thinking and stewing helped me come up with great answers but it didn't. With every lap I felt more angry and more ripped off.

I'd been excited about camp for months and now the whole thing was falling apart.

I couldn't play on the team I wanted to, I was separated from my buddies, my coach wasn't a Canuck and I still had endless drills to get through before the whole stupid week would be over.

How was I supposed to feel? Happy that nothing was going my way? Excited that Gunnar probably hated me for wanting to switch teams? Thrilled that Bosko was going to develop all kinds of awesome skills while I skated laps?

Gunnar blew the whistle for us to finish our final lap.

"Looks like you're on board," Patrick said, tightening the strap on his helmet.

"On board what?" I asked.

"The team. It looks like you're willing to give it a chance."

I stared at him. "Where'd you get that idea?"

He stared back. "You were hauling just now, Nugget. Tearing up the ice."

"So?"

"So, it looked like you cared."

I shook my head. "I don't."

"Well, Gunnar does. She was watching you and she looked pretty impressed."

I sighed. The last person I needed to impress was Katie Gunnar.

"Let's work on our passing," she said to the team. "Get into groups of three, and try to find people you haven't worked with before."

By the end of the day, we'd run a bunch more drills and I was still ticked off. And when Gunnar blew her whistle to another day with no actual playing, I didn't even care about camp any more.

Chapter Eight

Me and Colin both got a ride home at the end of the day from Mrs. Cavanaugh. Kenny and Colin talked about what an awesome time they were having at camp while I didn't say a word.

Day two, and *my* hockey camp was a total bust.

I stared out the window, wishing things had turned out differently, but knowing there was nothing I could do about it.

"What's your deal, Nugget?" Colin asked, as we turned onto my street.

"Nothing," I said, shaking my head.

"I guess I'd be looking the same way if I were you," Colin said.

"Man, I'm glad I'm on Holbrook's team," Kenny said. "We should play a game against you guys, Nugget."

"Yeah, right," Colin laughed.

"What's so funny?" I asked.

"Uh, what Kenny just said?" Colin laughed again.

Kenny nodded. "We'd smoke you guys."

"I think you mean girls," Colin corrected.

"You're hilarious," I said, turning back to the window.

"You couldn't play us, anyway," Colin said. "You haven't even played each other."

"Drills, drills and more drills," Kenny chimed in.

I couldn't argue with that, so I gritted my teeth until Mrs. Cavanaugh dropped Colin off, then pulled into my driveway.

"Thanks for the ride," I said, once I'd climbed out of the van. I swung my heavy bag onto my back and nodded to Kenny. "See ya."

I carried my bag to the front door, amazed I could even lift the thing, which seemed twice as heavy as it was that morning. Of course, I'd still had hope way back then.

As soon as I made it to the mudroom, I dropped the bag on the floor and walked into the kitchen. I was tired and thirsty and all I wanted was a big glass of juice.

Mum stood in front of me, her hands on her hips.

"What?" I asked, moving toward the fridge.

She took a step to her right and blocked me. "That sounded suspiciously like a big bag of hockey gear being dumped on the floor."

Here we go.

"That's because it was," I said, trying to pass her again.

She was too quick, especially after camp had totally worn me out.

"We've had this conversation before, Jonathan."

I sighed. "So do we have to have it again?"

She raised an eyebrow. "Apparently, we do. You know you're not supposed to treat your gear like that."

While she was talking, I walked back to the mudroom and unzipped the bag, half-listening to her as I pulled my

Canucks jersey and my stinky socks out of it.

"When you get home from practice, you —"

"Sort it and put the stuff that needs to be washed in the laundry room," I finished for her. I dropped the dirty stuff into the basket.

"So that you'll be ready for tomorrow."

"But that's the thing," I told her. "I don't think I'm going tomorrow."

"What?" Mum said, frowning.

"I might skip it," I shrugged.

"Skip what?" Wendy asked.

She always showed up when things were getting tense. It was like she had snooping superpowers.

"Hockey camp," I said, moving past her and finally making it to the fridge. I grabbed the carton of orange juice and pulled a glass out of the cupboard. A big one.

"You've got to be kidding," Wendy said, with a snort.

I turned to give her the most serious look I could. "Nope."

"You're going to skip the camp you *begged* to go to?" Wendy asked, reaching for the juice carton as soon as I was finished pouring my glass.

"No," I said, sitting down at the table.

"But you just said —"

"I'm not *at* the camp I begged to go to. I'm at Katie Gunnar's camp."

"This again?" Mum sighed.

"Yes," I told her. "This again."

"What's going on?" Dad asked, walking into the kitchen and intercepting the juice carton just before Wendy put it back in the fridge.

"Jonathan wants to skip hockey camp tomorrow," Mum told him.

"Really?" Dad asked me, looking totally surprised. "Are you sick?"

Yeah. Sick of the whole mess. "No."

"Then what is it?" Dad asked.

I shrugged. "You know."

"We don't know," Mum said. "You're going to have to explain, Jonathan."

"It's Katie Gunnar."

I told them about how she wouldn't let me switch teams and how we'd spent two whole days running drills instead of playing. Then I told them how much fun Danny Holbrook's team was having.

"It isn't all about fun," Dad said. "You're supposed to be learning, too."

He sounded just like Patrick.

"I know," I groaned.

"This camp wasn't cheap," Mum said.

"I know and I'm sorry, okay? I had no idea it was going to turn out like this."

"Regardless of how it's turned out, you talked us into sending you."

"Yeah but —"

"I'm afraid that you're going to have to see it through until the end."

It was really weird that the hockey camp I'd dreamed about for weeks was turning into a punishment. I was actually being *forced* to go.

"Yeah," Wendy piped in. "You can't just spend your whole life being a quitter."

"I'm not a quitter," I snapped.

"So prove it," she said, with a smirk.

My body was aching, I was tired of the conversation and

to top it all off, I was totally turned off by what I'd seen next to the orange juice in the fridge. We were having cabbage rolls for dinner.

Cabbage rolls. Could the day get any worse?

I couldn't leave the kitchen fast enough.

I left the three of them and headed upstairs, where I could feel sorry for myself in private.

A few minutes later I heard Mum leave to go grocery shopping and I knew Dad was working in the den. No matter how hard I tried to tune her out, I could hear Wendy talking on the phone (as usual).

So I kept to myself and I messed around in my room, kind of reorganizing. I moved my Ducette poster to the spot next to the window, being super careful not to tear the corners when I pulled out the thumbtacks. I re-arranged the books on my hockey library shelf, first by colour, then by size, from biggest to smallest.

I thought about re-reading one of them, but instead of being inspired by Gordie Howe or Gretzky, I had the feeling the stories of their lives would only depress me.

I couldn't imagine any of the greats being stuck in my crummy situation.

I listened to PUCK Radio for a little while. Stan Danielson was interviewing Matthew Crane, who played left wing for the Penguins. He was an awesome player and I wished that the Canucks had signed him when they had the chance.

When the interview was over, I looked up Crane's hometown of Glace Bay, Nova Scotia in my atlas. It turned out to be on Cape Breton Island, and I thought it was pretty cool that he was an islander, like me.

I wondered how many teams had been in *his* league when he was growing up.

And if his mum had ever signed *him* up for the wrong camp.

I doubted it.

PUCK Radio started to play a repeat of an interview I'd already heard, so I turned it off and looked around my room.

I had *nothing* to do.

I glanced at the Math homework sitting on my desk and decided I wasn't *that* desperate yet.

But I was still bored out of my mind, so I finally lay on the bed, tossing a puck into the air and catching it, over and over again. The whole time I was doing it, all I could think about was how much it stunk that I couldn't wait for the Christmas holidays to be over so I could get back to my old schedule of regular Cougar practices and games.

I couldn't believe I was ready to go back to school.

Well, maybe not school, but regular life.

The worst part of it was that hockey camp was supposed to be the highlight of the year.

I looked at my Jean Ducette poster and thought about what life must have been like for him at my age. He actually had to work on his family farm during the holidays and fit in hockey with his brothers whenever he could. He grew up in a tiny town in Quebec that didn't even *have* a rink, so he'd never played on Zamboni-smoothed ice until he was a teenager.

But he made it to the NHL.

He made it to the Canucks.

I knew I wasn't up against the same kind of odds as Ducette. I knew that being part of a team like the Cougars was pretty cool, and it wasn't something every kid who liked hockey could do in their own hometown.

Not every kid had a dad who'd been scouted by the Flames when he was younger, or a mum who was willing to get up way too early on winter mornings to drive him to practice.

"Nugget!" Wendy shouted. "Get down here!"

Then again, not every kid had a teenaged sister ready to explode every day.

"I'm busy!" I shouted back.

"Your weird little friend is here!"

I rolled off my bed and headed downstairs. My weird little friend? That could be just about anyone.

When I got to the front door, which was wide open, Kenny was standing there.

I turned to stare at Wendy, who was leaning in the doorway, stirring an organic yogurt.

"That's *Kenny*," I told her.

Wendy just shrugged.

"Kenny Cavanaugh." I pointed past him. "He lives right there."

Wendy scooped a spoonful of yogurt into her mouth and swallowed it before saying, "You little twerps all look the same." Then she disappeared into the kitchen.

"What's going on?" I asked Kenny, hoping he'd come to apologize for talking trash in the car.

"You left this in the van," he said, handing me my Gunnar jersey.

I knew I'd tried to drown it in my bag that morning, but it must have made it to the surface when I shoved my gear in after camp.

"Thanks."

"You wanna play after dinner tonight?" he asked. "I can see if some of the other guys are up for it."

I shook my head. "I don't think so. I'm pretty sore right now."

"She really worked you guys out, eh?"

"Yup."

Kenny seemed to realize I wasn't going to invite him in like I usually did. He looked disappointed.

"Okay, well I guess I'll see you later, Nugget."

"Sure," I told him, closing the door.

"You kind of gave him the brush-off," Wendy said, from the kitchen door.

I shrugged. "I didn't really feel like hanging out."

"Hmm," she said. "Want some yogurt?"

"No way."

"I know where Mum hid the ice cream," she said, with an evil smile.

"I'm going to guess the freezer," I told her.

She nodded. "Not in here, though. It's in the chest freezer in the garage under like, two tons of spaghetti sauce. You want some?"

Ice cream actually sounded pretty good. "Sure."

Within a couple of minutes, we were sitting at the kitchen table together, each working on a bowl of Neapolitan. Well, the chocolate part of it, anyway.

"Mum will be surprised when she opens it up and sees she's only got strawberry and vanilla left in there," I said, smiling.

"Serves her right for hiding it," Wendy said.

"And for buying such a lame flavour," I added, and my big sister actually *giggled*.

I hadn't heard that sound for a couple of years.

"Are you really going to bail on your camp?" she asked.

"It doesn't sound like I'm allowed to, does it?"

"Not really. Is it *that* bad?"

"Yes," I said right away, then realized it wasn't totally true. "It stinks that I'm not on Holbrook's team, but there's nothing really *wrong* with Katie Gunnar."

"So why don't you just make the most of it?"

"I don't know," I sighed. "It's the other guys. I watch them playing all day while we're working hard, then they make fun of our team and the fact that I'm playing with girls, and —"

"You weren't too happy about the girls to start with," she pointed out.

"I'm still not *happy* about it, but . . ."

"But what?"

I shrugged. "They're better than I thought they'd be."

"Really?"

"Yeah. They keep up with us just fine." I thought about Ashley and that speedy little Cara. "In fact, a couple of them are better than some of the Cougars."

"I'm surprised to hear you say that."

"So am I."

At that moment, the back door opened and Mum came in loaded with bags. When she saw the two of us sitting at the table with empty bowls in front of us, I thought she'd be mad. But she smiled and I swear there were tears in her eyes.

"I've dreamed of a moment like this," she said.

Wendy and I looked at each other, confused.

"Like what?" my sister asked.

"Seeing you two hanging out together, like friends."

Wendy frowned. "We're not *friends*." She pushed her chair back and carried her bowl over to the sink.

"Don't let me ruin it," Mum said, not realizing it was too late.

Wendy soaped and rinsed her bowl, then left it on the rack to dry. "I was just bored, okay?" she said, hurrying out of the room.

Mum watched her go for a couple of seconds, then sighed. "Teenagers."

"Yup," I sighed.

"So can you help me bring in the groceries?"

I followed Mum out to her van and we unloaded it in record time, thanks to a sudden rainstorm.

When we'd put everything away, she handed me a plastic bag.

"What's this?" I asked.

"A little something I picked up for you at the bookstore."

I knew it couldn't be the next volume of *Shoot* because the last one had only been out for a month or so (long enough for me to read it from cover to cover three times already). First I was curious, then I got excited, hoping it was the new biography of Sidney Crosby.

For the first time that day, I was grinning, but only until I pulled the book out of the bag. I was holding it upside down, but I could tell by the colours that it wasn't the one about Crosby.

When I turned it right way up, I saw that the cover was a photo of a bunch of girls in hockey uniforms, hugging each other.

I couldn't help feeling disappointed.

"Uh . . . thanks."

"It's the Olympic team," Mum said.

"Uh-huh," I mumbled. The book was called *Gold*.

"So?" Mum said, looking all excited. "Which one is Katie Gunnar?"

I looked at all of the faces and spotted her on the left,

looking even more excited than Mum. "That one."

She leaned in for a closer look. "Oh, she's cute."

Cute?

How had I ended up with a "cute" hockey coach? It was *so* wrong. Coaches were supposed to be "tough" or "brutal" or something. Not cute.

"Well," Mum said, "I just thought it the book might give you some inspiration, honey. Enjoy it."

She left my room and I put the book on my night stand. I had no interest in reading it. At all.

*   *   *

After the cabbage rolls that night, it was my turn to clear the table. I thought unloading the groceries might have counted for something, but that just wasn't the kind of day I was having.

When I was finished and the dishwasher was running, I wandered into the TV room, where Dad was watching the news.

I'd heard the names of the people the anchors were talking about, and I knew a little a bit about some of the countries they showed on a map, but not enough to keep me interested.

"We can switch to a game after this," Dad said, seeing that I was bored.

"There aren't any on tonight," I told him.

"Well, we'll find something to watch."

I leaned back on the couch, trying to ignore the sounds of my buddies heading up to Tulip for a night game.

While my teammates tore up the asphalt, I ran a load of hockey stuff through the laundry and watched *Wheel of Fortune*, feeling like I'd landed on "Bankrupt."

Chapter Nine

The next morning, I had to seriously drag myself out of bed, like it was a school day.

I'd had a rotten sleep, thinking about how things had been going at camp, and I spent a lot of time lying in bed, staring at the ceiling.

At about one in the morning, I thought of what Gunnar had said about kicking someone out of camp for a bad attitude. And that made me think about what Patrick said about me being no different from the guys who gave my Dad a hard time when he wanted us to do plyometrics at practice. Their bad attitudes had almost ruined the Cougars' season and torn the team apart.

Was I acting any different from them by wanting a different coach and having a bad attitude when it didn't happen? Was complaining about days filled with drills any different from the guys complaining about Dad's coaching?

Probably not.

And that gave me a lot more to think about.

* * *

I felt a little more awake after my shower, and was totally alert when I saw that Mum had made whole-wheat pancakes. They're way better than they sound, at least if you soak them with syrup.

"That's enough," Mum said, taking the half-empty bottle away from me.

It wasn't even close to enough, but I also knew I'd never win that battle.

As I ate my breakfast, I watched her pack my lunch. She made me a tuna sandwich (which I liked, but the guys hated, mostly because of the smell), then added a couple of oatmeal raisin cookies (which rocked), some carrot sticks (which didn't) and my favourite member of the apple family, Granny Smith.

"Can I have an extra juice box?" I asked.

"I've been putting three in there."

I needed something to trade, and obviously no one would go for the carrots. "Please?"

"No more juice," Mum said, adding a bottle of water to the mix. "You'll rot your teeth out, one of these days."

Geez.

I heard Mrs. Cavanaugh's van pull up.

"Have fun," Mum called after me, as I hoisted my re-packed hockey bag onto my back.

Yeah, right. *Fun.*

I took a deep breath before climbing into the van.

After all of my thinking during the night, I'd decided that a change in my attitude would probably go a long way. It was the kind of idea I never would have come up with even a couple of months ago. But when I'd thought about how I'd acted over the past couple of days, I was kind of embarrassed.

I *had* been a whiner.

And maybe it *was* time for me to man up.

The only way to find out if a new attitude would help was to try it out.

"How'd it go last night?" I asked Kenny, once I was buckled in.

"Good."

"Cool," I said, surprised that he didn't have more to say.

"We lost two balls in the woods and one went down the sewer pipe."

That explained it. "Too bad."

"And that was in the first ten minutes we were out there."

"*Really* too bad," I said, chuckling. I guess I hadn't missed out on much.

"Yeah, we called it a night." He turned around from the front seat to look at me. "Think you might play tonight?"

"I'll have to see how torn up I am by Gunnar's camp."

"Cool," he said, nodding. "It's always better when you're there, Nugget."

"Thanks, Kenny," I said quietly. And I meant it.

* * *

After I got changed in the locker room, I headed out to the rink to see if I could catch Gunnar alone. But the only person I saw was Ashley Bosko. She was wearing all her gear, but sitting in the stands and digging around in a purple purse.

Since we had a few minutes before camp got started, I climbed the stairs and sat down next to her.

"Hey," I said.

She turned to look at me. "Wow, the beast can smile."

"Beast?" I asked, laughing. "Me?"

"Yeah, you. That's the first time I've even seen your teeth. It's good to know you've got more than gums in there."

"Uh, thanks?"

She turned back to the purse and the digging. "I sense you're in a better mood today."

"Yeah. I'm trying out a new attitude."

"It's about time."

"Wow, you really are Bosko's sister," I said, shaking my head.

She stopped digging to look at me. "You don't think we're alike?"

"No way." I laughed.

"How are we not alike?" she asked.

"Are you kidding?"

"No. Tell me."

"I don't know. You're not a . . . ," I didn't want to finish the sentence.

"Gorilla?" she asked.

"No!" I choked.

She raised one eyebrow. "Oh, so you think I *am* a gorilla?"

"No!" I said, again. Thug, yes. Gorilla, no. "I just meant you don't *look* like Eddie and Shane at all."

"Well, I would hope not. Last time I checked, I was a girl."

"I know, but —" I could feel my face turning red. Everything I said was wrong! "Look, I —"

Ashley laughed. "Relax, Nugget. I'm just giving you a hard time."

I shook my head and sighed. "Of course you are. You're Bosko's sister."

"*One* of Bosko's sisters," she corrected.

"What?"

"There are two girls and two boys. Our younger sister is Casey."

"Are you serious?" It was like the Bosko family was taking over the whole town. Or maybe even the planet.

"Yeah. She's living with my grandma in Victoria while she goes to UVic."

"Cool," I said, then thought about that for a second. "Wait, you said younger sister."

"Yeah, she's ten."

I practically choked. "Your ten-year-old sister goes to university?"

"Only a couple of days a week," she said. "You think Eddie and Shane are Math geniuses? They've got nothing on Casey and Biochemistry."

I didn't even know what Biochemistry was.

"So she's a prodigy too?"

"Duh. Did you listen to anything I just said?"

I had a feeling I'd regret asking the next question, but I was too curious to hold back. "So, if all three of them are prodigies . . . what, uh . . . what happened to you?"

She gave me a long look before saying, "I got lucky, I guess."

"Lucky?"

"Aha! There it is," she said, pointing at me.

"What?"

"The face Eddie told me you make when you're confused. He said your mouth hangs open, like a flounder."

I closed my mouth, feeling my whole face turn red.

She laughed. "Anyway, my point is that I wouldn't want to be a prodigy. In fact, I wouldn't wish it on anyone."

"That's crazy."

"No it isn't. My brothers and sister are totally obsessed. They eat drink and breathe their subjects."

"Yeah, but they're *geniuses*."

She rolled her eyes. "I know what prodigy means, Nugget."

"I don't get it," I said, shaking my head.

"What can I say? I'd way rather have a bunch of interests than one total obsession."

I thought about that for a second. "But Eddie has hockey and Shane has rugby. Their whole lives don't revolve around math."

She rolled her eyes again. "Okay, so my brothers are both half brainiac, half maniac. It's still pretty obsessive."

"But if they're geniuses —"

"Do you know what Eddie's going to be doing next summer, while you guys are all out playing street hockey?"

"Playing with us?" At least, I hoped so.

"Nope. He'll be at Polytechnique."

"That doesn't even sound like English."

"Duh. It's French, Nugget. Polytechnique Montreal. It's a university where he's going to a math and engineering camp."

"Instead of playing street hockey?"

She nodded. "Now, try to tell me that being a genius sounds fun."

"I never said it sounded *fun*, I just —"

"I think it's a drag. I'm totally happy being normal."

"Well, normal might be pushing it," I joked.

She gave me a warning look, so I left it at that. Normal or not, she was still a Bosko and could probably pin me if I ticked her off.

She dug around in her purse again for a second or two, looking annoyed.

"What are you doing?"

"Looking for my stupid cell phone."

"You have your own cell phone?"

She stared at me. "What did I just say?"

"How old are you?"

"Why, do I need a licence to use it?"

"No, it's just —"

"Thirteen."

"And you have your own cell phone?"

"Are you *really* asking me again?"

"Sorry. I'm just . . . surprised."

She looked me over. "Well, going by what Eddie says, you're surprised a lot." She smirked. "Flounder."

"I'd rather you didn't call me that."

"I'd rather you helped me find my stupid phone."

I sighed and started hunting around the stands. "What does it look like?"

"It has a little screen on it and lots of buttons," she said, sounding almost as sarcastic as my sister.

Almost.

"I know what a phone looks like. I meant colour or whatever."

"It has a green case."

Just then, Katie Gunnar blew her whistle, letting us know it was time to get out on the ice.

And that's when I saw them.

I didn't recognize the three boys as the Watsons right away because they all looked totally different (well, their hair did, anyway).

"Warren," the one with the new buzz cut and the

Holbrook jersey said, pointing to himself. "I'm *Warren*."

The next brother had kept his dark curly hair the same as it had always been. "I'm Quinn."

"And I," said the last one, who had bleached his hair so blond it was almost white, "am Simon."

"Everybody clear, now?" Quinn asked.

We were all too stunned to say anything, so we just nodded.

The Watsons were putting an end to the confusion, once and for all.

* * *

We did the usual drills all morning, which drove me nuts.

But not as nuts as Cara turned out to be.

"Hey, Gunnar?" she asked, when we were taking a break. "Do you think we could play against Holbrook's team?"

What?

They had twice the guys that we did and only three girls! It would be a disaster, and I'd never hear the end of it if they beat us.

"I don't think so," Gunnar said.

For once, we were on the same page.

"Why not?" Patrick asked.

"Because I asked him about it yesterday and he turned me down."

"Why?"

Gunnar shook her head. "He . . . " she paused for a few seconds, like she was looking for the right words. "He has a bit of an issue with me coaching."

"Why?" Patrick asked.

"I don't know. He thought he was being paired up with another NHL player. A guy."

"So?"

Gunnar shook her head again. "Look, it doesn't matter. Let's get back to work."

* * *

I was sweating like crazy by the time we took our lunch break. Me and the Cougars climbed up to our usual place in the stands and sat down.

To my surprise, Gunnar and the rest of her team joined us.

I traded one of my apple juices for a Twinkie (and could practically hear Mum screaming from miles away). Patrick swapped some Doritos for a banana and everybody plugged their noses when I unwrapped my tuna sandwich.

It was like Mum was psychic and knew I'd make the Twinkie trade. The tuna stink was her revenge.

"Hey, Gunnar?" Cara said. "How did you get to play in the Olympics?"

"By plane," she said, smiling.

"You know what I mean."

"Well," she answered, taking a sip of water. "I played hockey as a kid, then all through high school. I grew up in a really small town in Manitoba, so I had to play on a boys' team most of the time. Then, I played at McGill University, in Quebec, and when the time came, I tried out for the Olympic team."

"And made it!" Cara shrieked.

Gunnar shook her head. "Nope. I was an alternate." She was quiet for a second or two. "I was disappointed. I mean, the Olympics had been my dream forever, and to get that close but not actually make the team was pretty rough."

"Did you want to quit?" Patrick asked.

"I thought about it," she admitted. "The next Olympics

was four whole years away and I wasn't sure I'd even make the team on a second try, no matter how hard I trained." She looked at each of us, then said, "But I decided that it was important enough for me to give it a shot. So I kept training with the 2006 team, showing the coach how dedicated I was and proving to the other players that I wasn't a sore loser. I didn't realize it at the time, but I needed to prove it to myself, too."

"So how did you end up at the Olympics?" I asked.

"Melanie O'Donnell tore her ACL and couldn't play." She frowned. "It was hard. I saw how upset she was that she wouldn't be able to represent Canada. I wasn't sure if I'd be her alternate, but Coach took me aside, told me how impressed she'd been with my work ethic and attitude, and she put me on the team."

"Cool," Cara said, smiling.

"It was," Gunnar said. "Like I told you guys before, winning that medal was one of the proudest moments in my life. And to do it again four years later?" she shook her head. "Who gets two chances like that?"

I was still thinking about what Gunnar had said when Tim pointed out that Holbrook's team was still out on the ice.

For the first time I'd seen, the three girls were actually skating. Of course, it was in a corner, playing keep-away by themselves, but at least they were out there.

"Aren't they breaking for lunch?" Tim asked Gunnar.

"They should be," she said, searching the ice. "Where's Holbrook?"

We all looked, and none of us could spot him.

"Hey," Gunnar shouted. "Aren't you guys taking lunch?"

Colin shrugged and shouted back, "Danny told us to play."

"Where is he?"

"He had to go," Kenny shouted.

"Go where?" Gunnar asked, sounding shocked.

The entire Holbrook team shrugged at once.

"When did he leave?" Gunnar asked.

"Maybe an hour ago?" Colin said.

"You've got to be kidding me. Take a break, guys."

They hesitated for a second, then started to skate toward us.

"He had to *go*," Gunnar muttered, scowling. "Unbelievable."

* * *

After lunch, we ran a couple more drills, and then I heard the magic words I'd been waiting for.

"How about a scrimmage?" Gunnar asked.

Yes!

"That would be awesome," I told her, as the rest of the players cheered.

Gunnar split us up into two teams. I knew it wouldn't be boys against girls, and that was fine. I'd seen some pretty sweet moves from the girls already.

My team was made up of me, Simon (who I could even identify with his helmet on, thanks to the white-blond curls sticking out of the ear holes), Patrick, Ashley Bosko, Cara, two other girls whose names I didn't know and Big Nose from Port Alberni.

"My name's Mark, by the way," he said, once he was standing next to me.

"Nugget," I told him, with a nod.

"You play right wing," he said.

"Cool," I said, smiling.

"No, I mean you usually play right wing. For the Cougars."

"Oh. Yeah, I do."

"Well, that's my position, too," he said. "I know it's your home turf, but —"

"Go for it," me and my new attitude told him.

Chapter Ten

We all got into positions that most of us didn't usually play, with a couple of people from each team on the bench.

Gunnar dropped the puck. It was game time!

Patrick was at centre and he snagged the puck as soon as it hit the ice. He spun around and passed it to me, at defence.

I charged down the ice, slipping right between two girls and deking Tim out a second later.

"I'm open," Ashley shouted from my left.

But Simon was open, too, and I knew for a fact he could score.

New attitude.

I took a deep breath and passed to Ashley. Her long ponytail swung back and forth as she dodged around two of the girls and got in great position to take the shot.

Then she stopped and looked from one side to the other.

What was she waiting for? An invitation?

I'd give her one.

"Shoot!" I shouted.

Ashley swung her stick, hard and fast. We all watched the puck whip across the ice and slide right between Tim's skates.

"I don't usually play goal!" he shouted to the rest of us, as soon as he'd picked up the puck.

Only a day before, I would have pointed out that he didn't usually play at all, but my new attitude made me zip it.

The next thing I knew, Jeremy's sister, Tonia, was hauling down the ice toward me and I suddenly remembered I was playing defence!

I bent my knees and tried to guess which way she'd probably go. But I had no idea.

In a split second, she zipped around me like I was standing still. Okay, I *was* standing still, but I'd thought I had a bit more time. Man, she was fast!

I spun around and saw her heading for the goal, which was manned by one of the other girls. But before she could pull back her stick to take the shot, Cara came out of nowhere, like a redheaded tornado, and stole the puck.

Yes!

She passed to Simon, who passed to Patrick, who took the shot. The puck bounced off the blade of Tim's skate and toward the boards.

Port Alberni Mark hustled to reach it first and when he succeeded, he passed to Ashley.

This time, she didn't hesitate at all. She just let loose a killer shot that Tim didn't stand a chance of stopping.

And he didn't.

"That was awesome!" I shouted.

"Yeah, awesome," Kenny echoed.

"Getting the girls to do the work for you, Nugget?" Colin called from the other side of the rink.

I was kind of ticked off, especially when a couple of the other Cougars on Holbrook's team laughed.

"Ignore it," Patrick said, as he skated past.

"But they —"

He shook his head. "Aren't worth the wasted breath, Nugget."

I knew he was right. Again. "Hey, Patrick?"

He turned around. "Yeah?"

"Sorry about . . . how I've been during camp."

"It's cool," he said. "I'm just glad to see the real you back today."

After about fifteen minutes, my team was ahead by four goals, so Gunnar decided to mix things up. She switched players so half of us stayed where were and the other half traded teams.

Coach O'Neal usually kept the Cougars on the same teams and in their own positions when we scrimmaged, so I was interested to see how Gunnar's plan would work out.

It turned out to be awesome.

* * *

At the end of the day, I got changed and packed up my bag in the locker room with the rest of the guys.

And I mean *all* of the guys. It turned out that the players from Port Alberni had been changing in the washroom because the girls were using the Visitors' room. So I invited them to use ours.

"What are they doing in here?" Chris demanded.

"Same thing we are," I told him.

"Yeah, well they don't belong in our locker room," Colin said.

I waited for Kenny to chime in, like he usually did, but he left it alone.

"They're part of *our* camp," Patrick said.

"So are the girls," Chris argued. "But I don't see them in here."

"But I sure see a lot of girl uniforms," Colin said, laughing.

Patrick, Mark and Tim were all wearing the Gunnar jerseys that arrived midway through the day and I wished I were, too. I'd wear mine the next day, for sure.

"It's a cool jersey," Quinn said.

"Yeah, and the girls are actually pretty good," Simon added.

"Oh, boy," Colin said, rolling his eyes. "Here we go."

"They *are* good," I told him. "They're fast and they make smart plays."

"Yeah, right," Colin said. "Gunnar's team couldn't play their way out of a paper bag."

What?

"Why would we *ever* have to do that?" I asked.

"You know what I mean," Colin snapped.

"No, we don't," Patrick said.

"I mean that your whole team stinks and these Port Alberni guys need to be somewhere else."

"Get over it," Bosko said, from the corner. "It's a locker room, for crying out loud."

"But it's our —"

"*Get over it,*" he said again.

That shut everybody up.

Bosko left a couple of minutes later, followed by Patrick, the Watson triplets (I mean, Simon, Quinn and Warren), Bedhead and Jeff, who was chewing on some kind of wrinkled up pepperoni stick.

When there were just a few of us left, the room got even

quieter, which was fine by me. I didn't feel like arguing with anybody.

I high-fived Mark and Skinny, along with the rest of the guys, on my way out of the locker room.

"See ya tomorrow, Nugget," Mark called after me.

My attitude change felt good, and I was happy that I'd figured out that I needed it on my own (except for almost every member of my team calling me out, that is).

Kenny and me walked down the hallway together and when we were almost to the front door I saw a flash of something green under the vending machine.

"Hold on," I said, dropping my bag and heading over for a closer look.

I had to get down on my knees to reach it.

"What's that?" Kenny asked.

"Ashley Bosko's cell phone," I said.

"Maybe she's still here," he said.

"Nah. I think she and Eddie go home together and he's been gone for a while."

"She can wait until tomorrow," Kenny said with a shrug.

I tucked the phone into the front pocket of my hoodie, remembering how hard she'd looked for it that morning.

I wasn't so sure a teenage girl could make it through a whole night without her cell.

Mrs. Cavanaugh spent the whole drive home telling us about the huge list of things she needed to get done, so it didn't sound like a stop at the Boskos' house was going to fit in. I quietly held Ashley's phone and waited to get back to my place.

When we got there, neither of my parents' cars was in the driveway. I thanked Kenny's mum for the ride and walked around the back of the house. I dug the key out from under the rock I was pretty sure the whole neighbourhood knew was fake and opened the back door.

I didn't even have to call out a hello to know that nobody was home. The house had that creepy quietness to it.

I unpacked my gear and loaded the washing machine, then went upstairs to change.

I stared at Ashley's phone and thought about how protective Bosko was when it came to her. Would he be mad if I waited until morning to return the phone?

Probably. He'd think I stayed up all night reading her texts, or something equally creepy.

Since Wendy wasn't around to give me a ride, I left a note on the kitchen counter and got my bike out of the garage.

It only took me about fifteen minutes to get to Bosko's house, which had a minivan, a pickup and Shane's old beater in the driveway.

I parked my bike, thinking about the fact that I'd never actually stepped onto the Boskos' property before. He'd been tutoring me forever, but we always met at my house or the library.

I had no idea what to expect. Before I met Ashley, I might have thought the Boskos lived in a gigantic cave. Or maybe a massive gym, where they all worked out, benchpressing their own body weight and snacking on nuts and bolts (and I don't mean the pretzel kind — I mean car parts and stuff).

But if there were girls in the house, that kind of changed things a bit. It made me curious.

I took a deep breath before ringing the doorbell, then waited almost a whole minute before I heard footsteps inside. Big, thundering footsteps, loud enough to shatter windows and crack pavement.

"I *said*, I'm getting it!" I heard Shane yell. He whipped the door open and stared at me. "Nugget. What are you doing here?"

I dug into my pocket for the phone, but before I could say anything, Ashley joined him in the open doorway, a surprised look on her face.

"Nugget? What are you doing here?" she asked.

"I've got your phone," I said, holding it up.

"Yes!" she shrieked, as I handed it to her.

"You lost it *again*?" Shane asked.

She waved it at him. "No, I didn't." Then she looked at me. "Thanks for dropping it off. Wanna come in?"

In? Like, *inside*? I thought about saying no, but Shane had already moved out of the way and the door was wide open.

I felt like a mouse being lured into a trap, but the curiosity had gotten to me.

I stepped into a living room that looked just like ours, except for the thousand or so trophies, plaques, ribbons and photos all over the walls, tabletops and bookcases.

"Whoa," I whispered.

"Dumb, isn't it?" Ashley said, grabbing my arm and pulling me toward the kitchen. "Want something to drink?"

"I guess," I shrugged, wondering how many of the awards she pulled me past belonged to Eddie.

"You should stay for dinner," Ashley said.

"What? Me?"

She shook her head and her ponytail bounced all over. "You eat, don't you?"

"Yeah, but —"

"So eat here. Mum always has way too much food."

Dinner at the Boskos'? Could I handle that?

Did I *want* to?

When we walked into the kitchen, Mrs. Bosko was reading a magazine at the kitchen table.

"Hey, Mum?" Ashley said. "Can Nugget stay for dinner?"

What?

"Oh, I . . . uh . . . " I stuttered.

"Sure," Mrs. Bosko said, barely looking up. She was as tiny and bird-like as I remembered, and I still couldn't believe those giant sons were hers.

"What do you want?" Ashley asked, opening the fridge door.

"Um . . ."

"How about a pop or something? We've got Coke, Sprite, Gatorade, Vitamin Water and . . . " she disappeared behind the door. "Grape juice."

"Water is fine," I told her.

I didn't even know Eddie was behind me until he said, "Nugget. What are you doing here?"

When Shane and Ashley had asked me the exact same thing, they'd just sounded surprised and curious.

Eddie sounded dangerous.

"Uh . . . I'm . . . uh," I stammered, unable to form a word, let alone a whole sentence.

I didn't have to worry about it, though, because Eddie walked away without waiting for an answer.

* * *

When we all sat down at the dinner table about half an hour later, Mr. Bosko (and his huge neck, as thick as a tree trunk) sat at the head, with Shane and Eddie on either side of him. I sat across from Ashley, in their little sister Casey's spot.

Mrs. Bosko brought in the meal and it wasn't the hard metal objects or power shakes I might have expected.

Instead, she carried in a pizza the size of our kitchen table.

That's when I remembered that she didn't cook.

Before the smell of the pizza even reached me, Eddie and Shane had each grabbed a quarter of it and Mr. Bosko was trying to lift the other half onto his plate.

What?

Mrs. Bosko disappeared into the kitchen again and came back with *another* pizza, just as big. She put it on the table in front of me and I took one slice.

"So," Mr. Bosko said, as I battled a long strand of cheese stretched between the tip of my slice and my mouth. "How is Math going?"

"Good," I said. I hadn't won a whole living room full of trophies, but I was doing well enough not to fail the class.

"And your other classes?" he asked, raising an eyebrow.

I remembered the way he'd looked at me and Wendy the day she rear-ended someone in Mum's minivan. Like we were the dumbest people on earth.

"Fine," I told him. "Social Studies is a lot of work this year, memorizing a lot of stuff, but everything else is okay."

He tilted his head, obviously interested.

"If memorization is giving you grief, perhaps you should try a mnemonic device."

"A what?"

The whole Bosko family looked at each other, then back at me, like it was the most ridiculous question they'd ever heard.

"A mnemonic device," Mr. Bosko said again. "Something to help your memory."

"You know, like the one for the order of operations," Shane said. *"Please Excuse My Dear Aunt Sally."*

Order of operations?

Who was Aunt Sally?

My tutor could tell when I was confused, so he jumped in.

"When you're doing a math problem with lots of parts, you have to do them in the right order. In Shane's mnemonic device, the p in 'please' stands for parentheses, then the e in 'excuse' is for exponents, then it's multiplication, division, addition and subtraction. My Dear Aunt Sally."

"Oh." That was supposed to make sense?

Mr. Bosko cleared his throat. "You could also use a device like visualizing something that reminds you of what you're trying to remember."

Right then I was trying to remember how to listen without my mouth hanging open like a flounder.

Who *were* these people?

"Other times," Mr. Bosko continued, "it's a phrase, like Shane's. Let's say you were going grocery shopping and needed to remember beets, mushrooms and vinegar. That's b, m, v."

"Be My Valentine," Ashley said.

"What?" I choked. Was she talking to me? I glanced at Eddie to make sure he wasn't lunging across the table to strangle me.

"B, m, v," Ashley said, rolling her eyes. "Beets, mushrooms, vinegar. Be My Valentine."

"Very nice," Mr. Bosko said, then turned to me again. "What are you trying to memorize?"

Did I really want to continue the conversation? I couldn't see a way out of it.

"All of our Prime Ministers. In order."

"Hmm," all of the Boskos but Ashley said at once, leaning back in their chairs.

It was nothing like dinner at home. At all.

"I always remember Tupper by thinking of Tupperware," Shane said.

"Nice start," Mr. Bosko said. "Let's see what we can do with visual clues."

"John A. MacDonald was first," Eddie said.

"You could think of a pillow or some other object, in the shape of a giant number one, covered in a tartan pattern," Mr. Bosko told me.

What?

"A Scottish tartan," Mrs. Bosko said. "Scottish, like MacDonald."

"Or you could visualize one Big Mac," Shane suggested.

Ashley sighed. "Okay, I don't think he's going to need a mnemonic device to remember his own last name, you guys."

They all stared at her for a second, then Eddie nodded. "Oh, yeah. Nugget McDonald."

"Duh," Ashley said, looking at me and rolling her eyes. "McDonald to MacDonald isn't much of a stretch."

"Next up, Mackenzie," Mr. Bosko said. "What do you think, Shane?"

I knew they were trying to help, but I kind of stopped listening.

Maybe Ashley was right, and being normal was way better than being a prodigy.

And when it came down to it, I was pretty impressed that she'd actually survived that household.

Chapter Eleven

The next morning, after I'd had my shower and smelled bacon cooking (yes!), the first thing I reached for was my Gunnar jersey. Sure, it was a wrinkled mess from being balled up in my bag, but that wouldn't stop me from wearing it. I was officially part of Katie Gunnar's team.

I didn't even wait until I got to the rink to put it on, like I normally would.

"That looks great, honey," Mum said, when I came downstairs.

I knew it did, because I'd already checked myself out in the bathroom mirror. "Thanks."

"So," she said, with a knowing smile, "you're enjoying camp."

"Definitely," I told her, then explained a little bit about the other Cougars making fun of our "girl team."

Mum shook her head. "You guys need to stop bickering over all of the silly little details. It's just hockey."

What?

"First of all, it's not just hockey, Mum. And second, it's

not me causing problems," I told her. "It's Colin and Chris."

She gave me a knowing look. "It's everybody."

I couldn't really argue with that, especially when I was trying to shove a huge spoonful of fruit salad into my mouth. Blueberry, strawberry, peach and banana all exploded on my tongue.

Tasty, but it needed a little extra kick.

When I finished chewing and swallowed the mouthful, I reached for the sugar bowl.

"No," Mum said, snatching it away before I could grab it.

"Just a little."

"That isn't a bowl of oatmeal, Nugget. Fruit is naturally sweet."

"So is sugar," I told her.

"Not going to happen," she said, putting the bowl in the pantry.

It didn't matter. I had a feeling hockey camp would be sweet enough already.

*   *   *

Kenny and I joked around the whole way to the rink, and when we dumped our bags in the locker room, I was glad to see Patrick and Tim gearing up next to the Port Alberni guys.

The first hour or so of camp was pretty awesome. I felt fast and strong when we did our drills. It was cool to know that the workout would help me during our afternoon scrimmage *and* when Cougar practices started up again next week.

Every now and then, I'd check for any sign of Danny Holbrook on the other side of the rink.

He wasn't there, and it kind of looked like Colin was running things. He had a whistle stuck in his mouth and was splitting everybody up into teams. The next thing I knew, they were scrimmaging. Again.

The girls were still playing keep-away by themselves, which looked super boring.

"It's too bad Holbrook isn't playing the girls," I said, quietly.

Mark looked as surprised to hear me say it as I was.

"Yeah," he sighed. "We hear about it every morning on the drive here. They're pretty ticked off."

I would be too.

"You guys carpool?" I asked.

He nodded. "One of them is my cousin."

"Cool." I looked to the other side again. "Where *is* Holbrook, anyway?"

"Who knows," Patrick shrugged. "Making another *important* phone call?"

"Or catching a morning meeting?" I suggested.

"Are you guys with us?" Gunnar asked.

I nodded when I turned to face her, noticing that she was checking out the other side of the rink, too.

It seemed pretty weird that Gunnar and Holbrook were both there to coach and while she was keeping us hopping with drills, the Heroes were left to be zeroes.

"I really think we should play them," Ashley whispered, from the other side of me.

"Holbrook doesn't want to," I whispered back.

"He's not even *here*," Ashley said.

"Yeah, but —"

"Can I help you two with something?" Gunnar asked.

"No, I, uh . . . " I felt Ashley elbow me, pretty hard. But that wasn't enough to make me ask. "No."

"I think we should play Holbrook's team," Ashley blurted out before I could stop her.

Gunnar shook her head. "Not going to happen. I already asked him, remember?"

"I know, but can you ask again? Those guys have been total show-offs all week."

"We need to put them in their place," Skinny Port Alberni said.

"Please?" Cara asked, and all of the other girls chimed in.

"Fine," Katie said, shaking her head and laughing. "I'll give it another shot."

We warmed up by skating laps and every time I got a view of Holbrook's team, I looked for their coach. I didn't see him until my fifth time around, and when I did, he was standing on the ice, texting while the guys played.

The morning passed by pretty fast and when we played some keep-away, I noticed the girls on my team were better than some of the boys. Not better than *me*, but some of the guys. Cara was one of the best players and Ashley was good, too.

I took a quick bathroom break, and when I came back down the hallway toward the rink, all of the light was blocked by a giant shadow. I panicked for a second, until I realized it was Bosko.

"How's it going?" I asked.

"You tell me."

"What?"

"I said, you tell me, Nugget."

What was that supposed to mean? "Uh . . . "

He leaned close and I felt like I was shrinking. "I've been watching you."

I cleared my throat. "I've been watching you guys, too. You don't seem to have much supervision."

"I'm not talking about your team, Nugget." He made a V

with his fingers, which he pointed at his own eyes, then at mine. It was kind of scary. "I've been watching *you*."

Yesterday, he was backing me up about the Port Alberni guys in our locker room and now he was "watching me"? It didn't make sense.

"What's going on?" I asked, hating the shake in my voice.

"You tell me," he grunted.

"I have no idea what you want me to say, Bosko."

"Do you like my sister?" he demanded.

"What?"

"You heard me," he said, stepping close enough that I could smell peanut butter on his breath.

"No, I don't like her. I mean, I *like* her, but I don't like-like her."

He snorted. "Like-like? What are you, nine?"

"You know what I mean. She's cool to hang out with and stuff, but no, I don't *like* her."

"So you aren't in love with her?"

Okay, gross. "No."

"Good, because if you were, I wouldn't be too happy about it."

"But I'm not," I reminded him. Then I started thinking about how he drooled over Wendy. "Wait a second. You're *in love* with my sister."

"So?"

"So how is that any different?"

He leaned in really close, so I could not only smell the peanut butter, but practically taste it. "Because Ashley is *my* sister."

I couldn't argue with that.

"Well, I don't like her, so you have nothing to worry

about," I said, edging past him to get back out on the ice.

"I'm still watching you," he called after me.

* * *

When we broke for lunch, I headed for the stands to eat, but I stopped when I saw Gunnar approach Danny Holbrook.

I couldn't decide what I wanted to happen. If we played his team and won, it would be awesome. If we lost, we'd never hear the end of it.

"Danny?" Gunnar said, skating up to him.

"What?"

"My kids would really like to play your guys this week. You know, just a fun game."

"They wouldn't have fun," he growled.

"What?"

"Listen, Gunnell —"

"Gunnar," she said, smiling tightly.

"Whatever. Look at the group you've got. A bunch of girls and some pipsqueaks."

I felt my face get hot.

"What's your point?" she asked.

"My guys will tear them apart."

"How do you know?" she asked. "You've barely even seen them play."

Whoa!

"Excuse me?" he barked.

"I'm not sure there is an excuse." She cleared her throat and I could tell she was nervous. "You're here to teach these kids new hockey skills and maybe some life lessons and —"

"Give me a break. I'm here because my agent told me to be here." He shook his head. "And I thought it was going to be high school kids, not . . . *this*."

She frowned. "Great attitude, Danny."

"What do you care?"

"I consider it a privilege to be asked to coach these kids."

"You would," he sneered.

Her cheeks turned bright red. "And why is that?"

"You're crazy enough to think you have something to teach them."

Katie took a deep breath and I could see that she was steaming mad. "Why don't you put your money where your mouth is, Danny? I officially challenge your team to a match on Friday afternoon."

"You *officially* do, eh?" He laughed. "No thanks."

"So you forfeit?" There was no nervousness in her voice, now.

He frowned. "No."

"Then Friday it is. Two o'clock," she said, and skated off before he could say anything else.

I had to admit, I was totally impressed.

I climbed the stairs, smiling to myself. Katie Gunnar was what my dad would call one tough cookie.

"What are you smiling about?" Ashley asked, as I climbed past the girls.

"Nothing," I said. "Just the fact that we're playing Holbrook's team on Friday."

"Seriously?" she asked, raising her hand for a high five.

I gave her one, then glanced up at the guys.

Bosko was looking like he might reach down my throat and pull out an organ.

I shook my head at him and whispered, "Gotta go," to his sister.

The last thing I needed was to get on the gorilla's hit list.

The fact that we'd kind of become friends while he tutored me didn't mean he wouldn't kill me.

I took a deep breath as I got closer to the guys.

"Nugget —" Bosko started, but I interrupted him.

"So," I said to the group. "It looks like Friday is game day." I looked at Patrick and Tim. "Us against them."

"Nah," Colin said, shaking his head at the same time and spraying us with spit-drenched cookie crumbs. "Holbrook will never let that happen."

"He already is," I told him. "We're taking you on."

"Ha!" Chris barked. "We'll wipe the ice with you."

"You think so?" I asked.

"Your team has more girls than guys," Kenny pointed out.

"Thanks for the news flash," I told him.

"You don't stand a chance," Bedhead said.

"We'll see about that," Patrick told him.

And suddenly I couldn't wait to play Holbrook's team. All week I'd been listening to them brag and watching them scrimmage, but they hadn't been paying any attention to *us*. They didn't know how fast Cara was, how much better I'd gotten at skating backwards or that Quinn was becoming an awesome stick-handler.

They'd been so busy acting like big shots, they'd forgotten to watch out for the underdogs.

I actually enjoyed my celery sticks, for once, and not just because Mum had added peanut butter. I was looking forward to putting the Holbrook team, including their coach, in their place.

"Anyone want my graham crackers?" Patrick asked.

"I'll take them," Bosko said, offering him an orange.

Kenny asked, "Are they supposed to be cookies or crackers?"

"Who knows?" Chris said. "Feel like giving up that Rice Krispie square?"

"No way," Kenny said, putting it in his lap for safe-keeping.

I watched the guys swapping food and when Bosko moved to a spot next to me, I tried not to panic.

"How's it going, Nugget?" he asked.

"Fine," I told him, taking a bite of celery. "Gunnar's actually a lot cooler than I thought. And tougher."

"I wish I was on your team," he said, quietly.

I didn't think I'd ever heard him say anything like that before. "Seriously?"

"Yeah. I'm here to have fun, but I also want to learn some new plays and moves, you know?" He shook his head. "Holbrook doesn't even want to be here, but these clowns are too star-struck to notice."

I looked at Holbrook's guys, who were all proudly wearing his name on their jerseys instead of their own.

I hadn't seen him coach anyone all week, and they were still acting like he was some kind of legend.

"Kind of nuts," I said quietly.

* * *

When I got home that afternoon, the first thing I did was grab *Gold* from my room. I carried it downstairs and got comfortable in Dad's recliner.

Before I opened the book, I took a good look at the picture on the cover. Gunnar and the rest of the team looked so happy and so proud of themselves, it made me want to know what it taken for them to get there.

The Olympics.

Gold medals.

I cracked open the book and started at the beginning.

Usually, I already knew a bunch of stuff about the team or person I was reading about, but this time, it was all new to me.

I read each of the player bios, and was surprised by how many of them were the only hockey players in their families. Then again, Gillian Apps had a father *and* a grandfather who were NHL stars. Now *that* was a hockey family!

What I was most surprised by was how many of them had to play on boys' teams growing up. Cutter Bay had had a girls' league for as long as I could remember, but when Gunnar's teammates were girls, there was nothing for them.

How weird would it have felt to be the only girl on a team? Never mind that it sounded like they always got stuck in goal.

Ugh.

I was amazed they'd stuck with the sport at all.

The book was so interesting that before I even realized it, I was almost forty pages in and really liking it.

"What are you reading?" Dad asked, sitting on the couch across from me with his newspaper.

I told him about the gift from Mum. "Did you know that women have only been playing hockey at the Olympics since 1998?"

Dad nodded. "I did. There were other events that didn't used to be open to women, too. Like the marathon at the Summer Olympics. Women didn't compete until 1984, which isn't that long ago."

I stared at him. "Yeah, it is."

Dad laughed. "I mean in the big scheme of things, Nugget."

I could see what he meant — 1984 wasn't a hundred years ago or anything.

"It's pretty cool to know someone who actually went to the Olympics," I told him.

"And won," Dad said.

"Twice." I thought about it for a second, the way Bosko had put it. "Gunnar's team beat every other team in the world."

"Pretty impressive," Dad said.

"Gunnar even scored the final goal for the gold medal the second time around."

"How is she doing as a coach?"

"Good," I told him. "She knows lots of stuff and she's good about spotting our weaknesses." I shook my head. "But I guess Holbrook's good at spotting *her* weaknesses."

"What do you mean?"

I shrugged. "He's been kind of a jerk. He didn't want his team to play ours because we have a bunch of girls on our roster and he kind of put Gunnar down for being a girl coach, too."

"And are the girls pretty good?"

"Yeah. Some of them are awesome."

"Well," Dad said, "I don't want to point fingers, Nugget, but you had a bit of an attitude about a female coach, too."

"I know," I sighed.

"You judged her the same way people have judged you for being small. You've spent your whole hockey career trying to prove to people that you're a tougher and better player than they think."

"Same as Gunnar," I said, feeling like I'd been a jerk, myself. Dad was right. I hadn't given her a chance at all. But at least I was making up for it.

Chapter Twelve

We all knew we had to work super hard, since the big game was just a day away.

We were all wearing our jerseys and even though the rest of our gear didn't match, we still looked like a unit.

A solid unit.

We skated lines for what seemed like forever and I wanted to stop for a break. I was sure my lungs would actually explode, but when I saw Ashley Bosko and Cara hanging in there, I pushed myself to keep going.

"Nice work, guys," Katie called out to us as we finished up the lines, totally out of breath and sweaty.

"Skate a couple of cool-down laps while I set up the cones."

As tired as I felt, I was also glad that Gunnar was taking the camp as seriously as we were. I was glad she had something riding on the scrimmage against the Heroes, too.

It was all about pride, for all of us.

All morning, we worked together, whether it was sharing shots on goal, encouraging each other to give it our best or just keeping the puck moving between us.

It was a lot of work, but it was totally fun, too.

Just like every other day, I kept an eye on what was happening across the ice, and just like every other day, the kids were running the show while Holbrook did his own thing.

I tried to imagine what it would be like to make it all the way to the NHL, retire after a pro career, and years later be asked to run a camp for kids who were dying to be around you.

And not care at all.

I honestly couldn't imagine it. Hockey was my life and if I had the chance to be a star way after my career ended, I'd be all over it. I'd be giving kids pucks that I'd taken the time to autograph myself. I'd tell stories about my days in the NHL. I'd give everyone tips on how to play better while making sure they knew they were doing a pretty awesome job already.

I'd be a *coach*.

Every now and then, I'd see Katie watching them too, and I had the feeling she was thinking the exact same thing.

"Next drill," Gunnar said, interrupting my thoughts. "We're going to work on backchecking."

Ugh. Definitely not my favourite thing to do.

We were supposed to break into pairs, so before anyone could ask me to be their partner, I asked Tim to be mine. I still felt bad about calling him nothing but a benchwarmer and I was pretty impressed about how he'd been playing all week. It seemed like the right thing to do.

"No, thanks," he said. "I'm with Patrick."

"Cool," I said, disappointed. Maybe it wouldn't be quite that easy to win him over after I'd been a jerk. And that was fair.

By the time I turned back to the rest of the team, they'd all paired off.

Except Ashley Bosko.

Uh-oh.

I glanced at her brother, who was busy re-tying his skates.

"I don't have cooties," Ashley said.

"I never said you did."

"So we're partners."

I nodded, hoping Bosko would take at least fifteen minutes with those laces.

Gunnar explained that the first two pairs would wait in the end zone circles on either side of the goal. When she blew her whistle, the first pair would skate around a cone closer to centre ice, one with the puck, the other back-checking. Once they got around the cone, the one with the puck would try to shoot on the empty goal. When she blew the whistle again, the second pair would go and the next sets would move into the circles to wait.

"Sounds easy enough," Ashley said.

"I hate skating backwards," I told her.

"Man up, Nugget," she said, laughing. "You'll be fine."

And, surprisingly enough, I was.

When Gunnar blew her whistle we got started, and thanks to the drill work I'd been doing all week, it was easy to concentrate on what Ashley was doing with the puck instead of getting distracted by my footwork.

Gunnar really knew how to coach!

I actually managed to steal the puck from Ashley and take the shot myself.

"Nice one!" Gunnar called out to me, then blew her whistle for the next pair.

"She's right," Ashley said. "You're a really good player, Nugget."

"Thanks," I said, lining up beside her to wait for out next turn. "So are you."

What?

"Nah." She shook her head. "I'm decent, but I'm not that good."

"Sure you are! You're fast, you always find an open space and your shooting is awesome."

She frowned at me. "Did my brother put you up to saying that?"

I gulped. "No! In fact, he'd probably try to strangle me if he heard it."

She rolled her eyes. "Well, it was nice of you to say, but I know I'm just average and I'm okay with that."

I totally disagreed, but I let it go.

I couldn't help thinking again about how weird it must be to feel like the only average person in a family packed with superstars.

It would be *really* hard, but Ashley didn't seem bothered by it the way I would be. She just kind of accepted it.

On our next turn, Ashley pulled a sneaky move and got the puck away from me. She missed the net, but not by much.

"Nice check," I said.

"You let me steal it."

"No, I didn't." It was the truth.

"Whatever. You don't have to pretend you stink just to make me feel good."

Pretend I stink?

"I *didn't*," I told her.

My attitude might have improved, but I still wanted to shine on the ice. Sure, I wanted Gunnar to be the one to notice my most awesome plays now, instead of Holbrook, but I still wanted them noticed!

* * *

For the rest of the morning, we kept up the pace, and when lunchtime finally rolled around I was dying for a break. And a sandwich. And a burger. And maybe a steak.

Just before we skated off the ice to grab our lunches, Gunnar told us she had something to show us.

We all crowded around her, and when we did, she pulled two velvety boxes out from behind her back. I knew what was going to be inside as soon as I saw them.

She opened the first case and there it was: her 2006 gold medal.

"Whoa," Patrick and Cara whispered at the same time.

"Can we touch it?" Ashley asked.

"You can wear it," Gunnar said, smiling.

I couldn't believe it!

She opened the second box, then we each took a turn holding one of the medals. I got the one from Vancouver in 2010, which was awesome. When I hung it around my neck, I was amazed at how heavy it was. I'd watched a whole bunch of the Olympics with my family on TV, but I'd never seen what the medals looked like up close.

It wasn't totally round, and it was kind of wavy, like water, instead of flat. There was some carving on it, but I couldn't tell what it was.

"Each medal was part of a big piece of art," Gunnar told us. "It's hand cut, so every one is unique."

"Awesome," I whispered.

Ashley had the 2006 medal from Italy, which was a perfect circle with a hole in the middle that the ribbon went through.

"They aren't the same for every Olympics?" I asked.

"Nope," Gunnar said. "Kind of makes you want to collect them, doesn't it?"

"Definitely."

I could tell that Patrick was dying to see it, so I pulled the medal from my neck and handed it to him.

"It looks good on you," Gunnar said.

"My own would probably look better," he said, grinning.

I turned and saw Danny Holbrook sneering at Gunnar and before I really thought about it, I skated over to him.

"It's too late to change teams," he said.

I didn't say anything, but skated in a slow circle around him, looking him over from head to toe.

"What are you doing?" he snapped.

I stopped skating and stared up at him, thinking about how mean he'd been to my awesome coach.

"Looking for *your* Olympic medals," I said.

"What?"

"Oh, I forgot," I said, smacking my helmet. "You don't have any."

I thought he would say something nasty, but he just shook his head at me, turned, and pulled his cell phone out. Typical.

"What was that all about?" Gunnar asked.

"The difference between a Holbrook and a hero," I told her, skating off the ice to enjoy whatever Mum had packed for me.

*   *   *

At the end of the day, I walked outside with Kenny, but instead of Mrs. Cavanaugh, Mum's minivan was in the lot with my sister behind the wheel.

"What's going on?" I asked her.

"Kenny's mum had to take their dog to the vet."

"Is Badger okay?" Kenny asked.

She stopped chewing her gum to stare at him. "Do I look like a vet?" Then she saw how worried he was and said in a much kinder voice, "I don't think it's anything serious. She didn't look upset or anything."

"Badger?" he asked.

"No." Wendy rolled her eyes. "Your mum."

"Cool," Kenny said, obviously relieved.

Wendy looked around to make sure no one had witnessed the two seconds she was being nice. "So are you dorks getting in, or what?"

I opened the sliding door and hoisted my bag inside, but Kenny hesitated for a couple of seconds. He knew all about Wendy's driving "skills."

"It'll be fine," I told him.

He took a deep breath, threw his bag into the back and climbed in after it.

"Just keep your eyes closed," I said. "Tight."

I couldn't wait to see his reaction when Wendy peeled out of the parking lot, tires squealing.

I was just about to jump into the front passenger seat when I heard Bosko say, "Hey, do you think we could get a ride, too?"

I turned around and saw that Ashley looked as surprised as I was. Bosko only lived two blocks away from the rink.

He pointed to the bag at Ashley's feet. "That's a lot of weight for my little sister to carry."

"Big sister," Ashley said, rolling her eyes.

"Well, you're smaller than I am."

That wasn't saying much, considering the guy was built like King Kong.

I'd seen him carry his gear like the bag was filled with marshmallows. He could have easily carried both home on one shoulder.

Never mind that I'd seen Ashley carry her own.

"Fine," Wendy said. "Whatever."

It took less than two minutes for us to drive to Bosko's house and in that time, he never even blinked. He just stared at my sister like she was some kind of a goddess.

And Wendy? She pretended to scowl the whole time, but I knew she loved the attention (or stalking, which is what I would have called it).

When she pulled into the driveway, she turned off the engine. "Since we're here, I'm just going to zip in and say hi to Shane," she said, hopping out of the van.

"Seriously?" Kenny groaned. He knew as well as I did that once those two got together, it was almost impossible to pull them apart. Especially their lips.

Gross.

"Do you guys want to come in?" Ashley asked.

I watched my sister walk through the front door and figured we didn't have much choice. There wasn't a whole lot to do in the driveway in the middle of a rain shower.

"Do you think it's scary in there?" Kenny whispered to me as we followed the Boskos.

"Nah," I told him. "It's fine."

He stopped walking and stared at me. "You've been here before?"

"Yeah. For dinner." I felt kind of cool saying it, like I'd done something super scary, like spending a whole night in a haunted castle or trick-or-treating at our principal's house.

He didn't say anything else while we walked up the path to the house, but I heard his breathing get a little faster.

As soon as we got inside, his eyes locked on that living room packed with trophies and awards.

"No way," he whispered.

"I know," I said, wishing I had a tenth of what the Boskos did.

"I'll get you guys something to drink," Ashley said. "Just follow me to the kitchen."

"I wanna check those trophies out," Kenny said, practically drooling.

She grabbed both of us by the arm and started to pull us down the hall.

"Ashley, is that you?" Mrs. Bosko called from the kitchen.

"Yeah. Me and some kids from camp," she called out, then said, "Come on, you guys."

"We should take our shoes off," Kenny said, starting to slip his off while staring at a section of the wall that was filled only with medals. Like, hundreds of medals.

"You can leave them on," Ashley said, sounding ticked off. "Let's get something to drink."

"I'm not thirsty," Kenny said, totally distracted.

"Ashley," Mrs. Bosko called. "I need some help in here."

"Just a second!" She tugged harder on my arm. "Let's go."

"*Now*, Ashley!" Mrs. Bosko shouted, sounding less friendly than I'd ever heard her.

Ashley let go of my arm and just stood there for a couple of seconds, like she couldn't decide what to do.

"Ashley!" Mrs. Bosko shouted again, even louder.

I hated to think what her next try would sound like.

Ashley sighed and headed for the kitchen.

"What are they for?" Kenny asked, walking into the living room for a closer look.

I followed him, curious as well.

"Math, rugby and hockey," I said, knowing that's what Eddie and Shane were into. "And probably some science stuff for their little sister."

"Ashley," Kenny asked, looking at the biggest trophy, which was taller than he was.

"Casey," I corrected.

"No," Kenny said, pointing. "Ashley."

"What?" I asked, moving in for a closer look.

The huge trophy *did* have Ashley's name on it. And so did the one next to it, and three of the plaques on the wall.

What was going on?

"Ashley, Ashley, Ashley," Kenny read, pointing at each award as he said the name. "Eddie, Ashley, Shane, Shane, Ashley."

"Are you guys coming . . . " Ashley started to say from behind us, then gasped. "What are you doing in there?"

I turned to face her. "Looking at all of *your* trophies."

She frowned. "They aren't all mine."

"Just the huge ones?" I asked. "What about being normal?"

She stared at me. "That's what I wanted to know."

"Normal?" Kenny asked, still checking out the awards. "This isn't normal."

"Why did you lie about it?" I asked, wondering how many dumb things I'd said in front of her. She'd probably told Eddie what a dork I was so the two of them could laugh at me behind my back.

Okay, that didn't sound like the kind of thing Eddie would do. But Eddie wasn't a liar and Ashley was, so how could I know for sure?

"Are you going to answer?" I asked.

"I wanted to be normal for like, five minutes, okay?" she said. "Do you know what it's like being a genius in a whole family of geniuses?"

Kenny and I looked at each other, amazed that she could ask us a question like that without laughing.

"No," I told her. "We have no idea."

"I feel like a freak, you guys. A total freak. And for once in my life, I wanted to be normal."

I couldn't understand that at all. I mean, all I'd ever wanted was to be a hockey superstar.

And she wanted to be normal?

I didn't get it at all.

Chapter Thirteen

I actually woke up feeling kind of bummed on Friday morning. It was the last day of camp, and even though I had the big scrimmage to look forward to, I knew that as soon as we'd played, it would all be over.

I was also bummed about Ashley Bosko lying to me. I couldn't understand why she'd done it, especially since I thought were, well . . . *friends*.

Man, was that a strange thing to realize.

I'd never had a girl for a friend before.

Of course, I'd never had a friend tell me a big fat lie like that and make me feel stupid, either.

While I was in the shower, I focused on hockey instead of the lying. Gunnar's team would finally have our chance to make the Heroes take back everything they'd said about how lame we were.

We had to win. We just *had* to.

But could we?

"Why so glum, chum?" Dad asked when he passed me coming out of the washroom.

"Last day of hockey," I sighed.

"You'll be back to the Cougars in a week," he reminded me. "And you've got a whole lot of street hockey to play in the meantime."

"I know," I said, nodding. But it wasn't the same.

After I was dressed in my sweats, I glanced at the Olympic book on my bedside table. Then I looked at my hockey library and realized something I'd never thought about before. None of my books were autographed.

I grabbed *Gold* and tucked it under my arm before heading downstairs.

Wendy was coming up at the same time. I didn't think I'd seen her awake so early in my entire life. Her hair was all messed up and at least half of the makeup she spent forever putting on every morning was smeared all over her face. The other half was probably on her pillowcase. Gross.

"Twerp," she grunted, as she brushed past me.

"Creep," I muttered back, quietly enough that she wouldn't hear me. As much as I wanted to stand up for myself, I didn't want to do it backed against the wall with my thug sister's arm pressed against my throat.

Been there, done that.

When I walked into the kitchen, the first thing I noticed was that there was no feeling of breakfast in the air. No smell of warm maple syrup. No sizzling waffle maker, oozing blueberry batter. No eggs scrambling. No toast . . . uh, toasting.

"I made oatmeal," Mum said.

Ugh. That would do it.

I didn't even try to hide my disappointment as I sat at the table and looked for a whole bag of brown sugar to dump on the lumpy stuff in front of me.

"I was hoping for something good," I muttered.

Mum heard me. "Well, there's good, and there's good for you."

"See?" I said. "Even you admit they're two different things."

"Eat, Nugget," she ordered.

So I did.

"Last day," she said, ruffling my hair, then lifting the book off the table. "How is it?"

"Really good," I told her, then chased my mouthful of mush with a big slurp of milk. "I'm hoping Gunnar will sign it."

"I'm sure she'd be happy to." She pointed to the laundry room. "Your jersey, socks and the rest of your gear are on top of the dryer."

"Thanks, Mum."

Maybe she'd be willing to sign the jersey, too. How awesome would that be?

I'd only made it through half of my oatmeal before I heard Mrs. Cavanaugh honk her horn in the driveway.

"Gotta go," I told Mum.

"You didn't finish," she said.

"It would be rude to keep her waiting," I said, hoping that would get me off the hook.

"Good one." She sighed as she handed me my lunch.

If she'd been in the mood to make oatmeal, I hated to think what kind of a nightmare was in that paper bag.

I grabbed my clean gear from the laundry room, shoved it into my gear bag and let Mum kiss me goodbye.

"Last day," Kenny said from the front seat, after I'd climbed into the minivan and buckled my seatbelt.

"Yup."

"We're gonna smoke you guys this afternoon."

"Kenneth!" his mother warned.

"What? We are." He shrugged. "It's a simple fact."

"We'll see," I told him, feeling like we had a decent chance of winning.

But what if we didn't?

How long would it take for my teammates to let it go? One week? Two?

No, we *had* to win. It was as simple as that.

* * *

When we got to the rink, it looked like we were the last ones there. Kenny and I rushed to the locker room and got changed as fast as we could.

When we were done, Kenny stared at my jersey.

"It's so weird to see you wearing that," he said.

"I think it looks pretty cool, and it *is* my team."

"More like your Girl Guide unit," Kenny laughed.

I stared at him, partly because I thought we were past the teasing about me being on Gunnar's team and partly because there was no way he came up with that comment on his own.

"Who said that?" I snapped.

"Me?"

"I don't mean just now. I mean who said it first?"

He sighed. "Chris."

"Pretty hilarious," I said, rolling my eyes.

Kenny shrugged. "We all thought so."

"Well, I don't think you guys will be laughing when you see what those girls can do."

"French braid their hair?" he asked, chuckling again. That is, until he saw my raised eyebrow. Then he cringed a little. "That one was Colin."

"Hilarious again," I told him, picking up my stick and heading for the doorway.

"I was just kidding, Nugget," he called after me.

"I know."

That was the whole problem. All the guys thought it was okay to make fun of the girls and think they couldn't play as well as we could. Even I'd been thinking that way for most of the week. But the truth was, I would have been happy to go up against any team in the Island League with Cara, Ashley and Tonia on my side.

I stepped onto the ice, just itching to give the guys a run for the money.

Of course, we had to get through the whole morning first. And skating laps was a good chance to concentrate on something other than the scrimmage.

"Hey," Ashley said, moving in next to me.

"Hey," I said, speeding up.

But she sped up too.

"I'm sorry about yesterday," she said.

"Me too," I said, pushing the pace a little harder.

She kept up. "I was just sick of being treated like a weirdo all the time, you know?"

Why wasn't she even out of breath? "Smart isn't weird," I told her, going even faster.

"But genius is," she said, still keeping up.

"No, it's —"

"You saw what our dinner table is like. Seriously, Nugget. Mnemonics? Who does that?"

"Hey, my family plays Scrabble and stuff," I said, knowing it was a pretty weak argument.

"I saw your face and I know for a fact you thought it was weird."

"No, I —"

"It isn't just you, anyway. None of the kids at my school like me."

"Maybe it's because you're a liar," I said. I cringed a little because it sounded meaner than I meant.

"This week is the first time I've ever lied about it."

"And how did that turn out for you?" I asked sarcastically.

"Fine, until you guys found out."

"What I don't get," I said, seriously panting as we went even faster, "is why you decided you had to lie to *me*. I didn't give you any reason to think I'd be a jerk about it."

"Good point," she said.

The next thing I knew, she was a metre ahead of me, then another.

What the heck?

I grunted as I lifted my legs faster and faster, mad that I couldn't reach her speed.

I skated as fast as I could, but there was no way I could keep up.

And my jaw practically hit the ice when Ashley Bosko lapped me at top speed.

She slid to a stop and let me catch up.

"What was that?" I asked, ticked off that she'd beaten me by so much.

"Fast," she said, shrugging.

"I noticed. What are you, a superhero?"

"I used to be a speed skater." She stared at me. "And I can tell by your face that you're ticked off I beat you."

"No," I lied.

"Sure you are. You struggled to keep up, you couldn't

do it, and now you're mad at me."

I didn't want to admit it, but she was right. "Maybe."

"I've made my point. Now you know why I was hiding the fact that I'm a prodigy, too."

And a super fast skater.

Wait a second.

"Have you been going slow at camp on purpose?"

She nodded.

"Why?" I didn't give her the chance to say anything, because I already knew the answer. "You wanted to be normal."

"Yeah," she said, nodding. "And it worked. For a while, anyway."

I was still having a hard time understanding why she wouldn't want to show off. Sure, I understood that kids got jealous and everything, but so what?

"If I could skate like that, I'd do it all the time," I told her.

"That's because you don't have to worry about making friends, Nugget. You've got a ton of them."

I didn't know what to say and Ashley didn't say anything else. She just kept pace next to me until Katie blew her whistle to start our drills.

For the rest of the morning, I thought about what Ashley had said. If she was willing to skate slowly to fit in at camp, what kind of things did she do at school so kids wouldn't be jealous of her? Did she pretend she didn't know answers in class? Act less smart than she really was? Blow quizzes or tests so people would like her??

I thought about Bosko, and how no one ever gave him a hard time about being a genius (sure, that might have something to do with the fact that he was also a giant who could crush them if they did, but still). I wondered if maybe it was different for Ashley because she was a girl.

I thought about the players in *Gold* who always got stuck in the net instead of other positions, and the ones who were made fun of by both guys and girls for being on a male team when there wasn't any other choice.

I looked across the ice and saw that the girls on Holbrook's team were stuck playing cards in their penalty box.

It wasn't fair.

None of it was fair.

As soon as there was a break, I skated over to Gunnar.

"How's it going?" she asked.

"Good," I said. "For me, anyway."

She raised her eyebrows. "Okay," she said, like it was a question.

"You know, I've been checking out Holbrook's team and I'm tired of seeing those girls left out."

Gunnar nodded. "I tried to talk to him about it, but . . . well, he's kind of old school."

"But you aren't," I reminded her. "And us players? We're so new school, we're still *in* school."

"Good point," she said, chuckling.

"I think those girls should join our team."

"Nugget, it's the last day of camp."

"I know, but . . . they should get to play in the game, too. With us."

It was kind of a risky suggestion, because I had no idea whether they were any good and it was super important that we *win*.

At the same time, it was suddenly super important to me that they play.

Gunnar looked like she was considering it.

"I want them to help us smoke the Heroes."

Gunnar smiled. "That would be kind of sweet, wouldn't it?"

"Totally sweet," I told her, skating back to the rest of my team.

* * *

I was definitely ready for a break when lunchtime rolled around. As I passed the Port Alberni guys on my way to the Cougars' lunch spot, I told them about the girls joining us and they both high-fived me.

I thought about how dumb it was that the Blizzard didn't eat lunch with Ashley or the Holbrook girls and realized that us guys were doing the exact same thing to the out of town guys. It didn't make any sense.

So I invited them to eat with us.

"Are you sure?" Mark asked.

"Yeah," I told him. "It'll be cool."

It wasn't *totally* cool, though. While most of the guys didn't have a problem eating with "the enemy," Colin and Chris gave them the cold shoulder.

"Anybody want my cheese and crackers?" Patrick asked.

I did! I peeked into my bag and groaned when I saw a bunch of cherry tomatoes, two cartons of milk, a granola bar and an egg salad sandwich.

Great.

"What do you have?" Skinny asked, holding up a PB and J on the squishy white bread Mum swore she would never buy.

"Nothing you'd want," I sighed.

"Try me."

I lifted the egg sandwich out of my paper bag and cringed.

"Egg?" he asked. When I nodded, he handed me the peanut butter dream.

"Seriously?" I practically choked.

"I love egg salad," he said.

I bit into my new sandwich like it was a chocolate bar. And it tasted almost as good.

While I was chewing, I looked at the other end of the stands, where the girls were eating their lunches together. I thought about inviting them over too, but the truth was, they looked totally happy hanging out on their own.

It was on the ice that they needed the invitation.

I sure hoped Gunnar would make it happen.

And she did.

After lunch, we had three new players on our side, all wearing brand new Gunnar jerseys and big smiles. In fact, one of them almost blinded me with the glare from her braces, but that was okay.

Gunnar quietly explained to our team that one of our players had suggested they join us, and when Ashley and Patrick both gave me questioning looks, I just shrugged.

But they knew.

"That was really cool," Patrick said, when we split up into teams for a practice scrimmage.

"Thanks for going to bat for my cousin," Mark said, slapping me on the back. "I should have done that myself."

"Yeah, I'm impressed," Ashley said, smiling. "You're a good one, Nugget."

Knowing what a jerk I'd been earlier in the week, I was happy to hear it.

* * *

I couldn't stop checking the clock every couple of minutes, and when two o'clock rolled around, I was totally ramped up and ready for battle.

Gunnar blew her whistle and both teams met at centre ice.

"You guys don't stand a chance," Colin said.

"Wait and see," I told him.

He glanced at our three new girls and laughed. "You're playing with our rejects, Nugget."

"Nope," one of the girls said. "We joined a new team, so we actually rejected you."

The rest of the girls giggled, and so did I.

Danny Holbrook just glared.

"Let's move on," Gunnar said. "We'll play three fifteen minute periods. Ready?"

We all cheered and skated to our own benches.

Gunnar listed her starters and I was glad to be one of them.

"Are we gonna do this?" Quinn asked.

"We've practically done it already," I told him. We'd done it in my head, anyway.

Us starters skated into position, and I eyed the competition, who didn't look nearly as serious as we were. Oh well, that was their problem, not mine.

I figured I'd be up against Colin at left wing, or maybe one of the guys from out of town. So when Eddie Bosko skated over and faced me across the line, I swallowed hard.

He was supposed to be right wing, like me.

Sure, we'd played against each other before, but that didn't mean I liked it.

I looked at the other Cougars out on the ice, getting ready to play against me.

It was kind of a spooky feeling, knowing that some of my best friends would be my enemies for the rest of the afternoon. I wondered how Bosko would feel when we played his old team, the Sharks, later in the season. He'd played with those guys for as long as I'd been teammates with Colin, Kenny and everybody else.

Then again, he hadn't been listening to his old teammates talk trash for a whole week.

I couldn't wait to wipe the ice with them.

I checked out Danny Holbrook, who actually looked like he was paying attention, for once.

That is, until his phone rang.

I shook my head as I watched him head for the bench to take the call.

"No way," I muttered.

"Tell me about it," Bosko said. "You definitely lucked out at this camp."

I totally agreed.

Gunnar blew her whistle once, then dropped the puck. Jeff McDaniel took possession and passed to Eddie in about half a second. I tried to check him, but he breezed past me like I was a ghost.

Part of me wished Dad hadn't made him play left wing when he subbed in as coach. Bosko didn't need the extra edge.

I chased after him, determined to get that puck, but when he deked out Simon and headed for the goal, it ended up being his own sister who stole it.

"Go, Ashley!" Cara shouted from the bench.

She was going, all right.

She whipped down the ice, dodging Chris and a Port Alberni guy so she could head straight for Bedhead at goal.

But Kenny got in the way.

"Nugget's open!" Patrick shouted.

Ashley glanced at me, then passed the puck.

"Nice pass!" Gunnar shouted.

I didn't have a clear shot, so I skated around the back of the net, knowing Bedhead hated that. I came in tight and took my shot, but he dropped to one knee and it bounced off his pads.

Nuts!

Kenny chased down the puck, then hustled across centre with no one covering him.

"Get him!" Tonia Simpson screamed from the bench.

Ashley took off like she was on fire and caught up with Kenny, but couldn't get the puck away from him. He went right and she stayed close to him, all the way to the boards, where it was hard to tell who was shoulder-checking who.

"Nice one!" Quinn shouted when Ashley came away with the puck.

She was back down the ice like lightning, and before I'd even crossed the centre line she was circling the goal.

But Bosko was right on her, taking jabs through her skates from behind.

It was battle of the geniuses, right before my eyes.

Ashley came out on top of this round, and when she saw an opening, she took the shot.

Bedhead blocked it with his stick, but before he could pass the puck to one of his defencemen, I swooped in and stole it.

I was back behind the net again, watching his helmet swivel back and forth while he tried to figure out which way I would come at him.

The right way, it turned out, when I slipped the puck right past him on the left.

It was hard to tell who on Gunnar's team was screaming the loudest, the boys or the girls.

"Lucky shot," Chris said, bumping me with his shoulder when he skated by.

"Lucky enough," I said, smiling. "One-zip, buddy."

"Not for long," he muttered.

Unfortunately, he was right.

The Heroes came back strong, scoring two goals in the next three minutes.

The guys went nuts, cheering, but I didn't hear anything out of Holbrook.

In fact, I couldn't even see the guy.

"Don't let them get to you," Gunnar shouted from the boards. "Shannon and Tim, take over defence."

I watched them race onto the ice while Patrick and Simon hit the bench for a break.

My heart was pounding. We were losing. Only by one goal, but they'd scored both of them so fast!

It turned out I didn't have to worry too much because in seconds, Ashley had the puck again and she was hauling toward the far goal.

"Nice hustle!" Gunnar shouted.

But Bosko was right on her tail, going after the puck.

"I'm open!" I shouted, in perfect position for a shot.

Ashley passed the puck high and fast, so I had to smack it down to the ice with my glove. In less than two seconds, I'd taken the shot.

In three, Bedhead had missed it.

"Nugget! Nugget! Nugget!" my teammates chanted from the bench.

It was seriously awesome.

By the time the first period was over, the score was still tied.

By the time we hit the end of the second, we were still two-all.

It was making me nuts!

We went into the third ready to "leave it all on the ice," as my favourite announcer, Dave Hodgkins, would say. And by all, I meant my heart and a bucket or two of sweat out would be left out there to get that win.

Late in the period, with only a minute left, Jeff passed the puck to Bosko and I was right on him, like a shadow. He moved left, I was with him. Right, I was there.

Neither of us said anything as we battled for possession. We just grunted.

He checked me against the boards, but that wasn't enough to stop me from coming after him. I wanted that puck more than I'd ever wanted anything in my life.

And I've wanted a lot of stuff over the years.

"Go, Nugget!" someone shouted.

"You can do it!" another voice called out.

"Come on, Bosko!" Colin yelled. "It's only Nugget!"

I'd show him "only Nugget"!

I got between Bosko and the goal, and the next thing I knew, I felt like I was in the middle of Gunnar's back-checking drill.

I'd always hated to skate backwards, but after she'd made us practise, it was no problem at all.

Just a metre or two away from the goal, I stole the puck! And I took off.

There was no one between me and a winning goal but Bedhead, and I was pretty sure he was ready for a nap.

I tore down the ice, hearing all of the shouts behind me. No one caught up with me.

It was the most awesome breakaway ever!

I went straight at Bedhead, and when I was ready, I let loose on that puck.

It flew through the air and, while I held my breath, soared right past Bedhead and into the net.

Yes!

We won!

My whole team was out on the ice in seconds, cheering and patting me on the back.

The Heroes looked pretty miserable, but that was fine with me.

"I'm so proud of you guys!" Gunnar said, pulling us all into a group hug in the middle of the ice.

I was so happy we'd won, I didn't even care that I was squished up with a bunch of girls.

Gunnar pulled out a big brown envelope. "I've got our team photos."

I thought way back to day two, when I'd been so desperate to switch teams. I hadn't even wanted to pose for the picture.

"Cool!" Cara said, reaching for one.

Gunnar passed them out to each of us. I stared at the picture, which showed everyone on the team smiling. Well, everyone but me and my bad attitude.

"Gunnar, do you have a pen?" I asked.

She pulled one out of her pocket, but before she could pass it to me, I handed her my photo.

"Can you autograph it?" I asked.

She grinned. "Absolutely."

"Mine too," Patrick said.

"And mine," Tonia added.

Pretty soon everyone was waiting for their turn.

"You *lost*?" a voice boomed from the other side of the ice.

I looked around and saw that it was Holbrook, talking to the Heroes while he shoved his phone into his pocket.

"You *lost*?" he said again. "To a bunch of *girls*?"

The whole rink was silent. I wanted to point out that there were guys on our team, too, but it didn't seem like the right moment.

"You!" he shouted. "Big guy."

He had to be talking to Bosko.

We watched Holbrook storm across the ice.

"What's your excuse?"

Bosko just stared at him.

"Answer me," Holbrook snapped.

"I don't think losing to a good team needs an excuse," he said. He shrugged like it was no big deal, but I could tell by the look on his face that he was ticked off. "But if you really want one, I could blame our poor excuse for a coach."

My jaw almost hit the ice.

"What did you just say?"

"I'll be right back," Bosko said, skating to the penalty box.

We all stood there silently until he came back.

"Who do you think you are?" Holbrook asked, as Bosko skated toward him.

Bosko just stared. "Who do *you* think I am?"

"What?"

"You don't even know my name, or the names of any other guy on this team."

I could tell by the looks on Colin and Chris's faces that he was right.

"Names?" Holbrook snorted. "I don't need to know your names. You think I wanted to be here, wasting my week with a bunch of kids?"

"Danny," Gunnar said.

He spun around to face her. "*You* can call me Mr. Holbrook," he sneered. "I was a pro, you know," he said, glaring at the rest of us.

"And she *is* one," Bosko said, pointing the felt pen he'd picked up in the penalty box toward Gunnar. "Gunnar, I was hoping you could sign my jersey."

My coach tried to hold back a smile, but couldn't do it.

"You've got to be kidding me," Holbrook said, but before he'd even finished, five more of the guys on his team were lining to have theirs autographed too.

It was awesome.

I watched Holbrook shake his head with disgust as he walked off the ice (the guy hadn't worn skates all week!), then watched Gunnar get the attention she deserved.

And while she was signing jerseys, I skated up to Ashley, then Cara, Tonia and the rest of the girls.

One by one, I had them sign my team photo so I could hang it in my bedroom.

I'm going to leave space on my wall for more photos. After all, the Winter Olympics are every four years, and I'm hoping that some of us will wear the red maple leaf someday.